He Was Going To Kiss Her.

But like a deer frozen by a set of headlights, she couldn't seem to move. Even when his lips touched hers, sending a slingshot of sensation zipping through her entire body, she still didn't try to escape. Then he wrapped his arms around her and there was no way she *could* escape.

His hands slid across her shoulders to her upper arms, and he gently pushed her a couple of inches away from him as he dragged his mouth from hers.

Keely whirled around so that her back was to him. "Ben, you have to promise one thing."

"And that is?"

"You won't kiss me again."

"I promise I won't do anything you don't want me to do," he said confidently, which left his options wide open. She'd wanted that kiss every bit as much as he had.

legs of her blue pin-striped jeans.

Dear Reader,

Check out the hot hunks on the covers of this month's Desire books. These are our RED, WHITE AND BLUE heroes, and they sure are something, aren't they? These guys are red-blooded, white-knight, blue-collar types, and they're guaranteed to make the hot summer nights even *hotter!*

Next month, we have a new title from Diana Palmer that I know you'll all enjoy. It's called *Night of Love,* and as an extra bonus it's *also* August's *Man of the Month* title. Also coming up in August are titles from Dixie Browning, Lass Small, Linda Turner, Barbara McCauley and Cathie Linz. Don't miss a single one.

And I'm still waiting for answers to last month's questions. What exactly do you like in Desire? Is there anything we can do differently? Do more of? *Less* of? No answer is too outrageous!

So, until next month, enjoy! And don't forget to let me know how you feel.

Lucia Macro
Senior Editor

KAREN LEABO

BEN

SILHOUETTE *Desire*®

Published by Silhouette Books New York

America's Publisher of Contemporary Romance

SILHOUETTE BOOKS
300 East 42nd St., New York, N.Y. 10017

BEN

Copyright © 1993 by Karen Leabo

ISBN: 0-373-05794-6

First Silhouette Books printing July 1993

All the characters in this book have no existence outside the imagination of the author and have no relation whatsoever to anyone bearing the same name or names. They are not even distantly inspired by any individual known or unknown to the author, and all incidents are pure invention.

® and ™:Trademarks used with authorization. Trademarks indicated with ® are registered in the United States Patent and Trademark Office, the Canada Trade Mark Office and in other countries.

Printed in the U.S.A.

KAREN LEABO

credits her fourth-grade teacher with initially sparking her interest in creative writing. She was determined at an early age to have her work published. When she was in the eighth grade, she wrote a children's book and convinced her school yearbook publisher to put it in print.

Karen was born and raised in Dallas. She has worked as a magazine art director, a free-lance writer and a textbook editor, but now she keeps herself busy full-time writing about romance.

One

Keely Adams dreaded meeting the man. He'd been described as a heavy-drinking gun-and-knife fanatic who alternately whipped and starved his daughter. Of course, the one doing the describing *was* the daughter, sixteen-year-old Tina Kinkaid, one of the high-risk students Keely counseled at J. C. Graham High School. Tina had been known to exaggerate.

Driving across Kansas City's Paseo Bridge on this fine April evening, Keely couldn't help but smile as she thought about Tina. Not that all of the students Keely counseled weren't special in some way. She had developed a fondness for each one of them. They were *her* kids, the family she would never have. But Tina, with her psychedelic clothes and her multipierced ears and a buzzed haircut that made Keely's own close-cropped brown hair look luxuriant by comparison, held a special place in her heart.

When Tina had first come to Graham she'd been a tough-talking, street-smart delinquent who didn't want to be in school at all. She was there only because a juvenile court judge had offered her the choice between a year at Graham or three months in juvenile detention.

Gradually, however, Keely had managed to penetrate Tina's tough shell to find the vulnerability and the keen intelligence within. The girl had made remarkable progress. She was pulling good grades, getting along well with teachers and students alike and was even working a part-time job after school.

But today Tina had taken a giant step backward. It was time, high time, to confront the father. Most children's behavioral problems could be traced directly to problems within the family, and Keely was determined to see for herself just what the girl's home environment was like.

Keely did know one thing about Ben Kinkaid: he hadn't shown a speck of interest in his daughter's progress at Graham. He hadn't once called to discuss grades or conduct or any of the other myriad problems Tina had harbored during her first few weeks as a sophomore at Graham. He didn't come to the school during open house. He hadn't volunteered to do anything.

Keely turned on Sixty-Eigth Street, then peered at the house numbers as she drove her white Escort down the winding, wooded lane. This comfortable suburban Kansas City sprawl, replete with split-level ranch houses, neatly trimmed lawns and late-model cars in the driveways, didn't jibe with Tina's poor-urban-girl-from-broken-home attitude.

Well, money didn't guarantee a happy kid, Keely reminded herself as she spotted the address and pulled up to the curb. And apparently the Kinkaids did have money.

There was a navy blue Porsche parked in the driveway, right next to the black Firebird Tina drove.

Keely rubbed her hands together as she made her way up the walkway to the front door, preparing for battle. She only hoped Ben Kinkaid would keep a grip on his temper. He had a vile one, if his daughter could be believed.

Tina herself answered the door. "Omigosh, Dr. Adams, what are you doing here?" she demanded, her soft brown eyes wide with surprise and maybe a touch of panic.

"I came to talk to your father. I'll set him straight about all this whipping and starving," Keely said with a skeptical lift of one eyebrow. "May I come in?"

Reluctantly Tina opened the door wider to admit Keely into the living room. "This isn't fair, you know," she mumbled. "You promised, the first time we talked, that you'd leave my dad out of things."

"Would you prefer that I ignore the situation and allow Mr. Showalter to expel you? He will, you know, if I don't recommend otherwise. And I can't recommend anything until I find out what your father has to say."

Tina started to argue further, but a deep-timbred voice drifted out from behind a set of louvered doors. "Tina? Who's here?"

"It's my guidance counselor, Daddy," she called back in a voice Keely could only describe as angelic. "Dr. Adams."

There was a telling silence before the anonymous voice was heard again. "Well, bring her in!"

"Okay, Daddy. I'll be back later."

Startled, Keely turned a puzzled face toward Tina. "You don't have to run off. We're not going to tell secrets about you. You're perfectly welcome to participate in the discussion. In fact, I encourage you to."

Tina opened the louvered doors, revealing a huge open area that housed a modern kitchen and a family room. "That's okay, I'd just as soon not," she said as she nudged Keely through the doors. With that she disappeared, almost like a wisp of smoke, leaving Keely alone with...with one of the most striking men she'd ever laid eyes on.

She wasn't sure what she'd expected him to look like— more like Tina, perhaps, who was small for her age, with dark hair, brown eyes and softly rounded features. There was nothing remotely small, soft or round about this man. He was at least six-two or -three, with shoulders that would challenge the width of any doorway and a wide expanse of what appeared to be a rock-hard chest. His face, too, was utterly uncompromising, a blending of planes and angles that might have been intimidating, had it not been for his look of almost childlike astonishment.

"Mr. Kinkaid?" Keely said, unwilling to believe at first that this was Tina's lazy, self-indulgent father. He certainly didn't show any of the signs of dissipation that might be expected. She'd apparently caught him in the act of wiping down the kitchen counters. "I'm Keely Adams."

He had apparently recovered quickly from his own state of bewilderment. "Yes, I'm Ben Kinkaid," he said, more wary now as she came closer. "I must say, Dr. Adams, you're somewhat of a surprise. You don't look at all like I pictured you."

"Nor do you," she murmured as she took his outstretched hand. He had a confident grip, firm but not crushing. "You've heard of me, then?"

"I've heard a lot," he said, faint disapproval evident in his voice. "Enough to know you're pretty tough on my daughter."

Oh, please, Keely thought, resisting the urge to roll her eyes. "I'm tough when it's called for," she said. "If you had objections to my dealings with Tina, you could have called me up anytime during the past four months to discuss the matter."

"Believe me, I was tempted to call," he replied, softening a bit. "But I couldn't. Please, sit down." He indicated one of the polished maple bar stools that pushed up to a roomy kitchen island. "Or we could sit in the den."

"This is fine." She had always preferred kitchens to any other room in the house, particularly when it came to sensitive discussions. There was something comforting and familiar about a humming refrigerator, a kettle on the stove, the lingering scent of baked goods from the oven, no matter whose kitchen she was in.

"Coffee?" he offered. "I just brewed a pot."

"Sure, that would be nice." She watched for a few moments as he took two cups from a cabinet and filled them both from the coffeepot. "What do you mean when you say you *couldn't* call me?"

"You," he said as he set a steaming cup in front of her, "sound just like a psychologist." His hands were large and tanned against the white ceramic cup. "Cream? Sugar?"

"Neither, thank you. I am a psychologist, so I can't help but sound like one, I suppose. And you're dodging the question. Maybe I don't blame you. I haven't even told you why I've come." She hesitated, wondering how best to broach the subject of Tina's latest indiscretion. "There's been some trouble with Tina," she began.

Ben's gold-green eyes became instantly more alert. "I didn't know there was a problem. Tina has led me to believe that everything at school is great."

"Her attendance is near perfect, her grades strong and she's been getting along better with both her teachers and the other students. In four months she's done nearly a year's worth of learning, so that she's no longer behind in her work. She's also been carrying around a six-inch switchblade.''

Ben did a double-take. "A what?''

"A big knife," Keely said, enunciating each word. "She claims she took it from your collection.''

"My collection, huh?'' He hitched one lean hip onto the bar stool next to Keely's. A deep groove had appeared between his eyebrows, and he raked a hand through his hair, which was thick and wavy, light brown shot through with gold. It reminded her of sunshine and shadows. "What else did she say?'' he asked, his muscles tensed as if to ward off a physical blow.

"Oh, quite a few things. She mentioned a parade of gruesome stepmothers, whippings, being locked in the basement, punishment by starvation, drunken rampages . . . any of this sound familiar?''

With every word she'd spoken, Ben Kinkaid's face had grown paler and his jaw had dropped farther. "Tina said all that?''

"I'm afraid so. Now, what *did* you mean when you said you couldn't call me?'' She didn't know why she was so determined to get an answer from him on that particular question, but it seemed important.

He gave her a wistful half smile. "You know Tina's background, right?''

"I know she chose to attend Graham rather than go to juvenile detention for stealing a car.''

"Right. Tina didn't want to go back to school under any circumstances, but I convinced her to give it one more try. She agreed on one condition—that I stay out of it. She didn't want me pressuring her to make good grades, or nagging her about homework. She promised to give it her best shot, and I promised to leave her alone.''

One of Tina's famous "deals," Keely surmised. The girl was fond of bartering her good behavior for whatever she wanted.

"I figured she'd be back in juvenile hall within a month. But somehow she made it work, without any help from me. So I continued my hands-off policy, difficult though that was. Judging from her report cards, she was doing fine—especially recently. But I guess she had me fooled, if she's carrying around a knife and lying. Damn, I thought those days were over.''

He looked so discouraged, Keely had to resist the urge to put a comforting arm around those broad shoulders. "Tina has made remarkable progress, and I truly believe we can overcome this setback. Did you know she's thinking about college?''

Ben nodded. "She's putting half of the money she earns into a savings account for college. I told her I'd pay for her education, but she still squirrels the money away.'' A shadow crossed over his face, sharpening his features. "At least, I think she's saving it. That's what she says, anyway. But you're telling me she's a liar.''

"Then all the things she told me about you are lies?'' Keely asked carefully, watching him as he watched her.

He scowled. "Of course they are! What kind of a father do you think I am?''

"That's what I'm here to find out. You...you don't lock her in the basement, do you?''

"Dr. Adams...Keely, let me show you something.'' He slid off his stool and motioned for her to follow.

She did so, though with some trepidation. Was he going to show her his knife-and-gun collection?

He led her back through the living room. She took more detailed note of the furnishings this time. The sofa and two armchairs were modest but comfortable looking, definitely masculine. Tina's books, jacket and a pair of her shoes were scattered around, and a half-empty bag of tortilla chips was wedged behind a pillow. The television had been left on, although Ben took no notice of it. Keely resisted the urge to reach over and shut it off as they passed.

Ben stopped at a door just off the living room. "This," he said with a dramatic flourish as he opened the door, "is our basement. After you."

Keely descended the dimly lit stairs, her heart thumping inside her chest. Was she crazy, secluding herself in a dark basement with a knife-and-gun nut? But after a few moments the lights blazed on, and the instant relief made her feel giddy and foolish. "Tina's room," she murmured.

The bedroom was a teenager's dream. In addition to being huge, it was filled with an amazing array of furnishings, most notably a king-size water bed and an enormous black enamel wardrobe stuffed to overflowing with clothes. The electronics—stereo CD player, color TV, VCR, Nintendo—were obviously state-of-the-art, much more sophisticated than anything Keely had in her own modest home. Posters of well-muscled, barely dressed rock stars and actors graced the walls and ceiling. An electric guitar, a keyboard and a set of drums were shoved into one corner.

"Even if I did lock Tina in the basement," Ben was saying, "which I can't because the door doesn't lock from the outside, I'd hardly call it punishment. Nor would it be possible for me to starve her. In fact, I'd say the opposite is true. I provide wholesome meals for the kid, and she turns up her nose at them and goes out for fast food."

Keely took another turn around the room, still trying to take it all in. Then she sat gingerly on the edge of the bed frame and folded her hands in her lap. She had no idea what to make of this place, the wealth of material possessions, or the man who had provided them for his daughter.

While Keely studied the room, Ben studied Keely. He had heard a lot about the school guidance counselor over the past few months. *She ought to be thrown in jail for criminal cruelty to children,* his daughter had said. This graceful, honey-voiced woman hardly resembled the witch Tina had described.

She was petite and small-boned, with flawless skin and alert blue eyes that seemed to take in everything. He sensed a quiet wisdom in those eyes, and a certain sadness, too. In contrast, her wispy cap of cinnamon brown hair and the pastel floral dress she wore projected an image of youthful innocence, though she was probably in her thirties. She had an unconscious way of fluttering her thick, black eyelashes that made his mouth go dry. Nope, he just couldn't envision Keely's slender, ringless hands wrapped around a broomstick.

"Need more convincing?" he asked after a few moments of silence. "You can search the house from top to bottom, and you won't find one gun or knife, except for the kitchen knives, of course. You can also check the refrigerator. There might be half a six-pack of beer in the very back, left over from a weekend at the lake. Other than that, there's no liquor in the house. And . . . did you say a parade of gruesome stepmothers?"

Keely nodded uncertainly.

"I can assure you I've only been married once, to Tina's mother."

"And where is she?" Keely asked.

Ben shrugged carelessly. "Who knows? She left us when Tina was seven. I won't deny that there have been other women in my life, but certainly not a 'parade.'"

None of them had stuck around long enough to become a stepmother, he added silently. Tina managed to scare them off long before that could happen.

"Well, I guess I owe you an apology," Keely said as she pushed herself off the bed. "I came here with a lot of preconceived notions about you that apparently aren't true. In my own defense, Tina can be pretty convincing when she wants to be."

"Yes, she can," Ben said as he led the way back up the stairs. He was wondering how much truth there was to the stories his daughter had told about Keely Adams. "Maybe I ought to send her to the Arts Magnet School next year and encourage her to train as an actress."

He'd been joking, but Keely's reply was very serious. "That may not be an option," she said as they returned to the kitchen and positioned themselves on their respective stools. "Tina is one step away from being expelled. Usually that's a given when a student is caught with a weapon in school, but I convinced our principal, Dan Showalter, to hold off until I could look into the situation."

"And did you talk to Tina?" Ben asked anxiously. "Oh, yes, of course. You said she claimed to have gotten the knife from me. Damn, you'd think after being caught with the knife, she wouldn't compound the offense by lying. Does she realize what's at stake?"

Keely nodded. "I don't condone her lying, of course," she said carefully, "but she was scared. She felt she'd been backed into a corner, and that's what made her revert to those old, negative patterns. Then, once she started, she just kept digging herself in deeper. I'm not so worried about that. I'm worried about why she thought she needed a knife in the first place. She says it's for personal protection."

"Protection from *what?*" Ben shot back, alarmed.

"She wouldn't say. But someone, somewhere, frightened her. You don't have any idea who?"

Ben shook his head. "Maybe someone at work?"

"Or a boyfriend," Keely theorized.

"That narrows the field down to about a hundred," he grumbled. "She has boys trailing after her like a pack of tomcats. So far she hasn't gotten serious about any of them, but maybe one of them has tried to push her too far."

"Uh, Mr. Kinkaid...Ben..." Keely hopped off her stool and began pacing the kitchen nervously. "What do you mean by 'serious'?"

"I mean she's not having sex."

"I, um, wouldn't be so sure about that. You know, things aren't the same as when you and I were in school. The peer pressure—"

"I *am* sure," he retorted hotly. "Don't be so quick to judge me by the stereotype of the bungling single father. Tina and I have had frequent, frank discussions about sex since she was eleven years old. She says she intends to wait until she's older."

"And we all know how sterling Tina's word is," Keely said dryly.

That stopped him. "You don't think she's actually engaging in..."

"Given the statistics, it's a good possibility." Keely seemed to choose her words carefully. Just the same, Ben was sure she knew more than she was telling. He supposed she had an obligation to protect Tina's privacy.

He scowled as he went to the coffeepot to pour himself a refill, needing to busy his nervous hands as he adjusted his daughter's image in his mind. "I've always encouraged her to be open with me."

"Don't blame yourself. No matter how open you've tried to be, there may be subjects Tina feels uncomfortable discussing with her father. I can promise you she's receiving accurate information, which puts her ahead of a lot of girls her age."

"What sort of advice do you give her?" he asked, trying to sound casual.

"I'm not allowed to tell you specifically what's been said," Keely replied. "I have to maintain confidentiality. But I can tell you that I try not to impose my morals on her. I simply encourage her to always consider the consequences of her actions."

"Somehow, at this moment that's hardly comforting," he grumbled. "Couldn't you just tell her that a lightning bolt will strike her down if she has sex before she's twenty-one?" He was joking, but the humor hid far bleaker emotions roiling around inside of him. His little girl was growing up and closing him out. He turned around and caught Keely's gaze, and for a brief, heart-stopping moment they shared a silent understanding. At some point in her life, someone she loved had disappointed her. "Do you have children?" he asked impulsively.

"A school full of them." Her answer was quick, pat and it hadn't revealed a thing. Apparently she didn't want to discuss her personal life. That was fine. She was here to focus on Tina and himself, after all.

"So, what do we do next?" he asked, dispelling the oddly intimate mood of the past few minutes.

"Well, I think Tina realizes the error in judgment she made by obtaining and carrying a knife. I pointed out several unsavory consequences she hadn't considered."

"But if someone is hassling her..."

"I gave her a whistle," Keely said. "It's something, anyway, and less lethal than a knife. I also suggested some ways she can avoid being vulnerable to unwanted advances. She shouldn't ever have to work alone in that video store, for example."

"It sounds as if you've been very thorough," Ben said, not quite sure how he felt about that. He thought of himself as a good parent, in spite of the problems he'd had with Tina. The fact that his daughter confided in someone else, accepted advice from someone else, bothered him a little.

"I did what I could," Keely said. "But I think we need to work together on this. Tina's come too far for us to lose her now. We'll have to tread very carefully to avoid undoing all the good that's been done."

Working together—Ben liked the sound of that. Pretty Keely Adams intrigued him, and not just because of her involvement with his daughter. "So what do you suggest I do?"

"Well, for starters, you should show more interest in Tina's schoolwork. I'm not talking about lecturing or nagging," she said quickly to forestall the objection he was about to make. "Just talk to her. Ask friendly questions. Offer advice, but don't insist she take it. Praise her if she does well on a test or whatever, but don't get angry if she does poorly. Focus on what steps she can take to improve the situation."

"You make it sound so simple. But it's not that easy to engage Tina in conversation. She's suspicious of the most innocent questions and immediately on the defensive. The moment I open my mouth, she accuses me of interfering, of trying to run her life."

"So? You're her father. You're entitled to exert some control over her life. As a matter of fact . . . well, has anyone ever pointed out to you that you've spoiled the girl silly?''

He could feel the hackles rising on his back. "Just what do you mean by that?''

"I mean, she's got enough clothes to stock the junior department at Saks and enough electronics to outfit the White House's media room. On top of that, she drives a brand-new sports car!''

"So? If I can afford to buy my child a few luxuries, why shouldn't I? It's one of the few ways we connect, and I like to make her happy. I also like to encourage her interest in music. And a second car is a necessity in a one-parent household, especially now that Tina has a job.''

"A bit defensive, are we?'' Keely asked.

Ben realized that he'd come off his stool and had practically been bellowing in Keely's face. Maybe he was defensive. But he still couldn't see what harm a few material possessions could do. His own parents had spoiled him pretty thoroughly, and he'd turned out okay.

He sank back onto his stool and took a sip of coffee. "Sorry,'' he mumbled.

"The things you buy Tina don't worry me nearly as much as another problem I see.''

"And that is?''

"I came here worried that you were too strict with Tina. I'm beginning to see that just the opposite is true. You're too permissive. You let her walk out of here without even asking where she's going or when she plans to return. Do you have any idea who her friends are? Does she have any curfews? Any ground rules for dating?''

"Look, maybe I am more permissive than the average parent,'' Ben said impatiently. "But I've tried all kinds of approaches with Tina. When I'm strict, she rebels and misbehaves that much more. But this past year I've been allowing her to make her own decisions, and for the most part she hasn't disappointed me."

"At sixteen, she *should* be allowed to make some decisions," Keely agreed. "But some decisions are too overwhelming for a child to make. She's looking to you for limits. She needs structure. She needs to be accountable. She needs to know you worry about her."

This was too much! "Look, lady, you can sit in your ivory tower and make judgments about my parenting skills all you want. You're a psychologist, after all, and I'm just an average guy. But you must *not* have any children of your own, because if you did, you'd know that sometimes those high-flying theories about how to raise kids have to be thrown right out the window. Sometimes you just have to do what works."

Keely was silent after his outburst—utterly, frighteningly silent. When she finally looked up at Ben, her eyes were unnaturally shiny, and her slender hands trembled as she pushed her coffee cup aside. "Yes, you're right," she said in an odd-sounding voice. "I don't have any children. I don't know what it's like to be a parent, any more than a kid peering through the glass outside a candy shop can guess what saltwater taffy tastes like just by the appearance."

Her oddly poetic response took the wind out of Ben's sails, and fast. What had he done to her? He'd wanted to knock her down a peg, perhaps, with his pretty speech, but he hadn't meant to hurt her. He touched her shoulder in silent apology. She felt fragile beneath his palm, and her muscles tensed, the way a cat tenses when it's not sure if you're friend or foe. "Look, Keely—"

"I think we've pretty well covered the territory," she interrupted, suddenly all business. She didn't respond to his touch, nor did she shy away from it. She simply pretended it wasn't there. "Now that I've discovered you're not Simon Legree, I'm basically satisfied. I'll recommend to Mr. Showalter that he give Tina one more chance, with your approval."

"Of course you have my approval," he said, awkwardly pulling his hand away. "Anything to keep Tina in school. I'll talk to her about the knife, just to make sure she understands. And I'll think about the other things."

She nodded. "Good night, then." She saw herself out quickly, before Ben could recover his wits or his manners.

Two

The flowers arrived in Keely's office just before lunch the next day—a huge basket of pink roses, daisies and miniature irises.

"Jeez, look at that!" Tina exclaimed from her desk in the corner of Keely's office. The principal had given her a three-day on-campus suspension in lieu of expulsion, and in a moment of insanity Keely had volunteered to act as "jail warden." "Who's it from?"

"I have no idea, it's none of your business and you aren't supposed to be talking, remember?" Keely said tartly. Part of Tina's punishment was that she wasn't allowed to speak.

Properly chastised, Tina returned her attention to her work. But her gaze strayed again to Keely as she opened the card.

Keely's heart raced as she read the message, printed boldly in the small space. "Thank you for saving Tina's

neck. Sorry for whatever I said that hurt your feelings.
Ben."

There was a P.S.: "I tried being firm. Questionable results. Could use more advice. Call me." It ended with a
phone number.

Why was he apologizing? Keely wondered, although her
confusion didn't blunt the surge of pure feminine pleasure she felt at receiving flowers from a very attractive
man. She should be the one to apologize. She had behaved badly last night, practically breaking into tears and
then rushing out of Ben's house as if her clothes were on
fire. He must think her a complete nincompoop. But he
had no way of knowing that he'd hit a sensitive spot when
he'd practically tweaked her nose with the fact that she was
childless.

It was silly for her to be so sensitive. She'd lived with her
sterility for more than ten years. But lately...

She tried unsuccessfully to put Ben out of her mind
during the rest of the day, but every time she turned
around the breathtaking flowers were there to remind her.
After she got home that afternoon, it took all her will-
power to wait until the evening to call and thank him.

When she did call, Tina answered the phone with a
breathless "H'lo?"

"Hi, Tina, it's Dr. Adams. Is your father home?"

There was a pause. "Yeah, he's here. You aren't gonna
tell him what I wrote in the essay, are you?" She was re-
ferring to a report she'd written about Shakespeare's
Othello, part of the extra work Keely had assigned. The
paper, while not exactly a scholarly interpretation, had
shown an amazing sensitivity toward the characters and an
honest attempt to relate the scenes in the play to real-life
situations and emotions. For all her outer toughness, Tina
Kinkaid's thoughts and feelings ran deep.

"No, I hadn't planned to mention it," Keely replied.

"Okay. Just a minute." As Tina handed the receiver to Ben, Keely could hear the girl's voice in the background: "You two gotta cut this out. You're making me very nervous."

Keely wondered what Tina would think if she knew Ben had sent those flowers. Although she had expressed curiosity several times during the day, Keely had managed to evade the questions.

"Hello, Keely?"

Keely's pulse quickened once again at the sound of his voice, so deep and warm. "Yes. Thank you for the flowers, but it really wasn't necessary. I was just doing my job."

"You went out on a limb and we both know it," he countered. "Now I understand you have to spend three whole days in the same room with Tina. Flowers were the least I could do. Do you like them?"

The question took her by surprise, especially because Ben sounded so anxious. "Why... why, yes, of course. What woman wouldn't appreciate a beautiful spring bouquet?"

On the other end of the line, standing in his kitchen, Ben frowned thoughtfully. Keely was being carefully impersonal in her answers, he noted, friendly but not in the least flirtatious. He wondered whether her caution was due to punctiliousness, or if she just plain wasn't attracted. He thought he'd seen a flicker of something other than professional interest in those wise blue eyes of hers, but he might have been mistaken. He hadn't tried to read a woman in that way for quite some time.

"You wrote on the card that you needed further advice," Keely said. "I'm glad to help out any way I can, but last night you weren't exactly grateful for my interference."

He winced as he recalled his angry response to her suggestion. "Let's just say I was taken off guard, and I overreacted. But after I thought about it, I realized that you must have lots of experience with troubled kids, and that maybe I ought to consider your recommendations with an open mind. In fact, last night I took your advice, or at least a small portion of it. I was very firm with Tina when she got home."

"And it didn't go according to the textbook, is that it?"

Ben hesitated. His confrontation with his daughter actually had gone better than he'd expected. "It's all so complicated," he said with a nervous laugh that wasn't at all feigned. "It's difficult to go into details over the phone."

"A lack of privacy?" Keely guessed.

"Yeah, that's it," he said, grasping at the excuse she'd provided. "Could we get together one evening to talk? Maybe over dinner?"

"Yes, I think that's a fine idea," she agreed enthusiastically. "In fact, why don't the three of us get together? I could throw some burgers on the grill and then, in a comfortable, relaxed atmosphere, we could help Tina set some goals, maybe do some role-playing—it could be very helpful."

That wasn't precisely what Ben had had in mind. "I was thinking of a strategy session. Why would we want to invite the, er, opposing forces?"

"Tina's not the enemy," Keely said, sounding just this side of outraged.

"Oh, for pity's sake, I didn't mean that."

"I certainly hope not. I really think some family counseling might do more good than a strategy session," Keely reasoned.

"She won't agree to it."

"Ask her."

He sighed. "All right. How about Saturday night around seven?" He held his breath, expecting her to reply that she was busy. This was already Thursday.

"Saturday would be fine." She gave him her address, and then concluded the call in a businesslike fashion.

Ben hung up the receiver, feeling vaguely disappointed. The conversation had left him dissatisfied. His initial goal had been to take some positive steps toward helping Tina—and that part had worked out all right. But he'd found himself also wanting to communicate with Keely as a man to a woman. Judging from her response, he wasn't making much headway.

True, he was out of practice when it came to the opposite sex. The intricacies of male-female relationships, with their ever-changing rules and ever-increasing risks, had become more trouble than they were worth in recent years. But had he completely forgotten how to communicate to a woman that he was interested? If a forty-dollar basket of flowers didn't do the trick, what would?

He was mulling over several interesting possibilities when he noticed with a jolt that his daughter was standing not four feet away, staring at him with sharp, accusing eyes.

"What are you trying to do, ruin my life?" she demanded.

"What do you mean?" he countered as he frantically reviewed his side of the conversation, wondering how much Tina had overheard.

"You and Dr. Adams. I heard you. You're getting together with her to plot against me."

"On the contrary. Dr. Adams suggested we all get together for some family counseling."

"You mean the three of us?" Tina asked suspiciously.

Ben nodded. "Saturday night."

"No way! I'm not wasting a Saturday night in some dumb therapy session."

Precisely what Ben had predicted—and could he blame her? He was a little uneasy himself over the idea of family counseling. But this was important, he reminded himself. Tina's problems had to be his priority. "What time would be more convenient?" he asked. "We can reschedule."

Tina folded her arms and assumed a mutinous expression. "You guys are gonna make me do this, aren't you."

"No. It's up to you."

"Then I don't want to."

"Okay." He turned back toward a simmering pot of spaghetti sauce he'd been neglecting.

"You don't seem too upset," Tina observed.

"Not upset, but disappointed. Given the recent troubles, I was hoping you'd be more willing to work together with Dr. Adams and me. Your whole future depends on what happens these next few weeks and months."

"Daddy, I know I messed up," Tina said, softening a bit. "I'll talk to Dr. Adams on my own. I'll see her every day if you want. I just don't want to talk to the two of you together. It makes me nervous."

"Why? We're just trying to help."

"Then why do I feel like you're plotting against me?"

Ben tried, and failed, to suppress a smile. "I'll make a deal with you. Dr. Adams and I won't talk about you at all when I go over there for dinner."

Tina started to open her mouth to object when the light dawned. "You mean you're still gonna see her Saturday night? So it'll be like...a date?" she asked in a voice filled with despair.

"I'm allowed to do that, aren't I?"

"But you haven't in ages. I thought you were through with that. You're too *old* to date. You two are acting like you're teenagers or something."

"No, if we were acting like teenagers I'd take her parking and try to score in the back seat." He watched Tina's face closely for a reaction, but all she did was roll her eyes.

Maybe "parking" was outré these days, he mused. Or maybe it was the term "score." Nothing turned Tina off faster than evidence that her father was hopelessly unhip. "I'm merely going to Keely's house for dinner," he continued. "And since you're included in the invitation, I wouldn't call it a date. And anyway, who says I'm too old to date? Even your grandmother dates."

"She goes square dancing. That's different. Daddy, if you've got this sudden urge to go out with someone, why does it have to be Dr. Adams?"

"What's wrong with Keely Adams?"

"She's the school counselor. That makes her almost like a *teacher!* What if someone finds out?"

"No one's going to find out unless you tell them."

"Oh, Daddy, you don't understand!" Tina wailed. She ran to her room and slammed the door.

Ben shook his head. Sometimes he was convinced an alien had come down from space and taken over the body of the sweet little girl he'd raised.

Maybe when she cooled off, she'd change her mind and come with him Saturday night. Part of him hoped she would. But another, unfatherly part of him prayed she wouldn't.

As she formed a half-dozen hamburger patties with nervous hands, Keely realized she was hyperventilating. She consciously took several slow, deep breaths. There was no reason to have an anxiety attack. True, it wasn't every day that she scheduled a family counseling session in her living room, but in this case she felt it was warranted. Her home would be neutral territory for both Ben and Tina. Plus, with the familiar trappings of a Saturday night cookout all around them, they might feel more comfortable.

It all made perfect sense. Then why couldn't she relax?

Face it, Keely, her inner voice scolded. It wasn't the counseling that made her nervous. She'd been involved in much stickier family situations than this one. It was the man himself, Ben Kinkaid, whose mere presence in the same room made her skin tingle.

She'd been physically aware of him from the very beginning, even when she was ready to believe the worst of him. After she'd come to understand more about his true nature, the awareness had only increased. She'd been acutely conscious of every gesture he made with his strong, competent hands, every nuance of emotion in the revealing expressions on his face.

Although they'd hardly touched in a physical way, the encounter had seemed unusually intimate for two people who'd just met. And now she'd arranged to spend an entire evening with him. Thank goodness she'd thought to invite Tina, or she might really be worried.

When the patties were molded to her satisfaction she put them in the refrigerator, then stepped out onto the deck to check the fire in her charcoal grill. The coals were coming along nicely. Another ten minutes and it would be time to cook the burgers. Now, to get herself in presentable order...

She was heading toward the bathroom, intending to make last-minute adjustments to hair and makeup, when the doorbell rang. Just her luck, they were early! She shrugged and abruptly switched directions. They would just have to take her as she was, faded lipstick, wind-blown hair and all.

She wiped her hands on her apron, then swung the door wide, ready to give her guests a cheerful greeting that hopefully would set the tone for the evening. The greeting stuck in her throat. Ben Kinkaid stood on her front porch, looking absolutely delicious in casual khaki trousers and a soft polo shirt the color of freshly churned butter. He held a bottle of wine in each hand. And he was positively alone.

"Tina?" Keely squeaked, much to her chagrin.

"No, I'm Ben. Tina's the short one with all the ear-rings, remember?"

I mean, she didn't come with you?"

"I told you she wouldn't. May I come in?"

"Oh, of course. I'm sorry." She stepped aside to allow him entrance as her heart started to race once again. She wished Ben had called to warn her that he'd be coming alone. Then she could have better prepared herself. As it was, he'd taken her completely off guard.

He held out both bottles of wine, one red, one white, for her inspection. "I never know what goes with hamburg-ers."

"Technically, red, I suppose." She examined the labels with more thoroughness than was warranted, giving her-self a much-needed chance to compose herself. "But I'd prefer the white, I think. Really, it wasn't necessary to bring wine."

"Few pleasurable things in life are 'necessary,' Keely," he said. The deep timbre of his voice sent a shiver from the base of her spine to her scalp. "Besides, it's rude to show up at someone's house for dinner empty-handed. If you'll direct me toward your corkscrew, I'll open the white."

"In the kitchen." She could already tell that her attempts to keep this evening on a light but professional level were doomed to fail. Just like the morning glory vines in her backyard, Ben's forceful personality was sending out questing tendrils toward the fertile soil of her soul, and she was allowing them to take root.

He followed her through the modest living and dining rooms to her small but efficient kitchen. Wordlessly she opened a narrow drawer and produced a fancy brass-plated corkscrew.

"Nice," Ben said, admiring the object with a low whistle. "Are you a wine connoisseur?"

She laughed at that. "Not exactly, although I do enjoy a glass now and then. The corkscrew was a present, many years ago." A wedding present, as were the seldom-used wineglasses she pulled from the top shelf of a cabinet. She quickly rinsed off the thin layer of dust and dried them as Ben busied himself opening the bottle of Chardonnay.

She set the glasses before him. "I'll go put the burgers on," she said, excusing herself. The sooner she got this show on the road the sooner it would be over. That was what she wanted, wasn't it? To survive the evening with her emotions intact? Give Ben the advice he sought, then get him safely out the door?

She was looking forward to a moment's respite from his overwhelming physical presence as she stepped out onto the deck with her plate of burgers, but he soon followed her, carrying two glasses of wine.

"This is really nice," he said, admiring the view of her small fenced yard, which was just greening out. In a few weeks it would be a riot of color, but right now it just looked lush and well tended.

"Thank you," she said, genuinely pleased with the compliment, for she was proud of her little green space.

"Gardening is my hobby, I guess you could say. I find it so relaxing."

"Therapy for the therapist."

"That's it, I suppose." She set each of the patties onto the grill, where they emitted satisfying sizzles. "How about you? Do you have a hobby?"

"I run, although it's not really what I consider an enjoyable activity," he said as he handed her one of the glasses. "I do it because it's the fastest, most convenient way to get exercise, and I do it no more than I have to—thirty minutes, three times a week."

"Even if you don't look forward to it, it probably does your mind more good than you think," she said, gratified to be on a safe topic about which she could speak confidently. She took a sip of the wine. It was crisp and dry and surprisingly cold. Maybe that fancy Porsche of his had a built-in ice bucket. "Physical exercise is a fantastic stress reducer," she continued. "And it's great for creating a positive self-image, especially if it helps you keep in shape—which in your case it obviously does."

The words were out of her mouth before she could consider how they sounded, and afterward she wished she could bury her head in the sand. Here she was, trying her best to maintain professionalism, and she'd just told Ben he had a nice bod.

"You obviously speak from experience." His statement was even more provocative than hers had been, especially when he accompanied his comment with a bold, head-to-toe appraisal. His gaze lingered longer than was polite at the top button of her white cotton blouse, then practically caressed her as it moved across her apron and down the legs of her blue pin-striped jeans.

She blushed. Her fair, translucent skin had always been one of her best features, but it had one disadvantage. Anyone could tell instantly when she was embarrassed.

"I work out at a health club, somewhat sporadically," she admitted, turning away to scrutinize the burgers, which unfortunately didn't seem to need a bit of attention. She took a long sip of wine and waited until the heat had receded from her face. When she turned toward him again, he was smiling as if he'd discovered some secret about her.

She wasn't sure she liked that. Her secrets were her own, and she shared them only with extreme caution. Ben hadn't yet earned her trust. She didn't want him privy to any but the most public facts about her.

Her mind searched for a safe topic. Even the subject of Tina seemed too personal at the moment. Mentally she groped, finally coming up with an appropriate, if pedestrian, question. "So, what kind of work do you do?" she asked as she settled into one of two deck chairs.

"I build swimming pools."

"Oh, Kinkaid Pools! Tina once mentioned something about you having rich customers, but she didn't get specific."

He shrugged. "That's what I do. It's a family business, but Tina—" He cut himself off.

"Yes?"

"Um, I think the burgers need turning."

"Oh." How easily he distracted her, she marveled silently as she flipped the patties. At least she hadn't burned them. When dinner was once again in order, she strolled to the edge of the deck and leaned her elbows on the railing, wondering what to do next. She hadn't engaged in enough dating over the years to be adept at small talk. But maybe with Ben, small talk wasn't necessary. Their silence now wasn't uncomfortable.

He followed her to the railing, propping his elbows next to hers. They gazed out over the yard for a few quiet moments.

"Peaceful," he said. "I like this neighborhood. Funny, I've lived in Kansas City all my life and I don't recall running across this area before."

"Not much of a demand for swimming pools around here," she said. "You were saying, about Tina?"

She didn't miss the fact that his fingers tightened around his wineglass. "Please. I enjoy so little peace. Let me linger in this serenity a while longer." He'd meant to make a joke, Keely knew, but as before, the humor hid far deeper emotions.

She was tempted to let it slide, to enjoy a quiet dinner and allow the wine to warm her blood and relax her muscles, which it had already begun to do. But the psychologist in her wanted to strike while the feelings were there, near the surface.

"Is it painful for you to talk about Tina?" she asked.

"Not painful. Just...unsettling. And frankly, though I honestly love my daughter, I've had about all I can take for one week."

"But that's what you came here for, to talk about her," Keely said.

He made no reply to that, but his silence spoke volumes.

"You did, didn't you?" she tried again, almost desperately.

"I promised Tina we wouldn't 'plot' against her, as she puts it. Besides, I'd rather talk about us."

"Us?" she repeated rather shrilly. "There is no 'us.'"

"But there could be." He looked at her then, leaning a few inches closer so that she could make out the individual flecks of gold in his eyes. Her chest tightened, and she took a deep breath, inhaling the essence of him, filling herself with his scent, his aura.

He was going to kiss her. The realization startled her, but like a deer frozen by a set of headlights, she couldn't seem to move. Even when his lips touched hers, sending a slingshot of sensation zipping through her entire body, she still didn't try to escape. Then he wrapped his arms around her, and there was no way she *could* escape.

For a few crazy moments she suspended her rational mind and allowed herself just to feel—his warm mouth pressing hard against hers, eliciting a response she couldn't suppress; his hands on her back, her neck, his fingers sifting through her already-tousled hair; his hard body pressed wantonly against hers. His subtle but tempting scent became entwined with the pleasant trace of mesquite smoke from the barbecue grill.

Just when she thought she would pass out from sensory overload, he began, slowly, to release her. His hands slid across her shoulders to her upper arms, and he gently pushed her a couple of inches away from him as he dragged his mouth from hers.

She whirled around so that her back was to him. With his handsome face safely out of her range of vision, the vestiges of control returned, along with rational thought. "I think you should leave," she said.

Ben sighed. "I will, if you really want me to. But what did I do that was so wrong?"

"You came here under false pretenses. You said you had problems with Tina when you really just wanted..."

"I do have problems with Tina. I tried to persuade her to come tonight, but she wouldn't."

"You could have called and canceled."

"And leave you with all these hamburgers? Besides, why should we waste a perfectly good Saturday night sitting at home when we can have dinner together?"

His cajoling produced a grudging smile from Keely. "You still should have been up-front with me."

"If I'd called and asked you out on a date, would you have accepted?"

She paused before answering. "Probably not."

"So you see?"

"I see where Tina got some of her sneakiness."

He came up behind her and put his hands on her shoulders. "I never lied to you. If it'll make you feel better, we can talk about Tina."

To Ben's surprise, Keely emitted a small laugh. "Actually, I've about had my fill of her, too. She's been in my office all day for two days straight."

"She's driving you crazy, huh?"

"A little," Keely admitted.

"Then what do you say that for tonight, we ban the subject of Tina? We'll relax and talk about all kinds of things that have nothing to do with teenagers."

"Mmm, do you know how long it's been since I've had a serious conversation with an adult that *didn't* involve teenagers?" She slipped out of his light grasp and went to the grill, where the hamburgers were smoking ominously. She flipped them onto a plate before they could char.

Still, she was far from relaxed. The stiffness of her movements told Ben that. She wasn't comfortable with the situation.

He was wondering what would put her at ease when she spoke up again. "Ben, you have to promise one thing."

"And that is?"

"You won't kiss me again."

"I promise I won't do anything you don't want me to do," he said confidently, which left his options wide open. She'd wanted that kiss every bit as much as he had.

Three

Somehow Keely made it through dinner. She even enjoyed it to a certain degree. The combination of a juicy hamburger, crisp white wine, a fine April breeze and Ben's company was heady stuff.

They sat outside at a picnic table, amid the fiery rays of the dying sun, and talked about everything from local politics to the music they'd listened to in high school. As Ben waxed nostalgic about a teenage flame and the ecstasy of slow-dancing with her at a school dance, Keely watched his hands and his mysterious green-gold eyes, and she could easily imagine herself as the lucky girl, her arms wrapped around his wide, football-player's shoulders, swaying to a ballad under crepe paper clouds and glittery stars.

She could recall no such moments from her own adolescence—only a few still-vivid daydreams. Back then she'd been small, mousy and studious, and she hadn't attracted much attention from the boys.

"I was a wallflower," she admitted.

"You? No way."

"Honestly," she said, hoping desperately to suppress the infuriating blush that threatened to creep up her neck. "Short, flat-chested redheads just weren't the rage at my school."

"You're not a redhead," he objected, although he pointedly looked at her breasts. It was as if he'd also said, *You're not flat-chested, either.*

Keely ran her fingers through her short, reddish brown hair. "It got darker," she said with a shrug. Then she added mischievously, "Time takes care of a lot of problems."

She should have known not to push her luck. He might have promised not to kiss her, but his hot gaze was almost more arousing than the touch of his mouth had been. She was treading in waters way out of her depth. Not only was she out of practice with men in general, but even in the heyday of her careless youth she hadn't toyed with a man this complex. For all his seeming good nature, Ben Kinkaid was dangerous to any woman, particularly one as attracted as she was.

A sudden gust of cool wind played havoc with their paper plates and napkins. Keely blessed the distraction as she made a lunge for her plate before it became a Frisbee.

"The temperature's dropping," she said with a small shiver as she collected the debris from their dinner. "Let's go inside."

She half hoped he would take that as a cue to leave. But then she glanced at her watch and stifled a groan. There was no way he could gracefully head for the door when it wasn't even eight o'clock yet.

In fact, he didn't appear as if he wanted to go at all. He whistled tunelessly as he collected the almost-empty wine bottle and their glasses and followed her through the sliding glass door.

Ben helped her put away leftovers and clean up. He seemed oddly at ease in the kitchen. Her ex-husband wouldn't have been caught dead washing dishes.

Egads, couldn't she compare Ben to someone more recent than a man she hadn't seen for ten years? She was frighteningly out of touch where men were concerned. It hadn't mattered much to her before.

It shouldn't matter now, she told herself firmly. The only thing she needed to concern herself with was shooing Ben out of her house at the first opportunity and reclaiming a safe, professional relationship.

Of course, she couldn't reclaim something she'd never had.

"Deep thoughts?"

His words made her jump, and she realized she'd been silent, lost in her own meanderings, for an unsociably long time. Another hazard of spending too much time alone, she supposed. "Nothing deep," she fibbed. "Just reviewing my grocery list. Sorry." Her hands fluttered in search of something to do, finally grabbing on to the wet barbecue tools Ben had just washed.

"Liar," he murmured. She turned her head in surprise. He was smiling, and again he had that knowing look about him, as if he could guess things about her that she'd rather keep hidden.

"What do you mean?" she countered, rubbing furiously at a spatula.

"No grocery list could produce such a thoughtful expression."

Since it was no use arguing with him, she conceded the point. "I'm entitled to my thoughts, aren't I?"

"Yes." He took the spatula, now drier than the Sahara, and the towel out of her suddenly limp hands. "You're going to rub the stainless steel right off of it," he teased. Before she could object, he had untied her apron, whipped it off her body and hung it on a drawer pull.

She felt ridiculously vulnerable without the wisp of checkered cotton guarding her lower torso. Nervously she smoothed her jeans over her hips and thighs. "Let's sit down in the living room," she suggested. Even to her own ears she sounded awkward.

Ben grabbed the two freshly washed wineglasses, the corkscrew and the bottle of burgundy, and followed her.

"More wine?" she asked.

"I'd like some more," he said mildly. "You're welcome to join me... or not." *But you could use a little loosening up.* He hadn't said it, but Keely could almost hear the words. She saw them in his eyes.

"Just because I asked you not to kiss me—" she began, but he interrupted her.

"I have no intention of plying you with alcohol so I can have my way with you," he said, sounding faintly amused. "But I do wish you would relax."

"It's hard to relax with you looking at me like that."

"Like how?" he asked innocently as he busied himself uncorking the wine.

"Like I'm a fat worm on a hook and you're a hungry bass," she blurted out.

"I can't help how I look at you," he said matter-of-factly. "I find you quite beautiful—and nothing at all like a fat worm."

She laughed despite the wretched turn this conversation had taken. "Well, I suppose you don't really look much like a fish, either," she admitted.

The cork came out of the bottle with a satisfying pop. Ben set the wine on the coffee table to breathe, then threw out his next questions as casually as the rest of the disturbing things he'd said. "Why don't you want me to kiss you? Are you seeing someone?"

"No," she answered quickly, then wondered why she hadn't latched on to the perfect excuse he'd provided.

"Why, then?"

They were both still standing in the middle of the room. Keely took a couple of steps back, then sank onto the coral-colored love seat. Belatedly she wished she'd chosen another resting place. "I don't want to compromise my work with Tina," she said.

It was a valid excuse. But Keely knew Ben wasn't buying it, not for a minute. He didn't even have to say anything. He just lifted one eyebrow, a more effective technique than the whips and chains of the Spanish Inquisition.

He was forcing her hand, and she didn't like it one bit. But she didn't see any way out of it. She would have to give him something akin to the truth, although not all of it. There was one secret he wouldn't wring out of her.

"I don't intend to have children," she said evenly. "I deal with children all day long. I see the problems, feel the hurt. I don't need to come home to that every day as well."

Ben stared at her, trying to fathom her meaning from that incredibly revealing face. Unless he'd missed something, he hadn't asked her to have his child. "How does your decision not to have children relate to my kissing you?"

"It doesn't, directly. But it does have to do with my attitude toward men." She paused to study her fingernails.

There was more, Ben was sure. He sensed she would get around to a full explanation if he just gave her a little space. So he sat down in the chair opposite her and waited.

"I married when I was very young and naive," she continued, slowly, as if weighing each word. "We both agreed that we didn't want children. I thought it was an ideal relationship—until Jeff changed his mind. Having children became almost an obsession with him. And when I wouldn't relent, he divorced me."

Ben's first reaction was white-hot outrage that any man could do that to Keely. But he bit his lip and remained silent. The story wasn't over.

"I had a couple of other relationships after that, but both times they fizzled when the man found out I didn't want children. Once I got over the rejections, I decided I couldn't blame those guys. It's only natural for a man to want to live on in posterity through his offspring, pass on his genes, that sort of thing." She made a dismissive gesture with her hand.

"And you haven't kissed a man since?" he asked incredulously.

"Well, I wouldn't say that. But I don't allow myself to get involved. It's just not worth the pain. There's a certain look in a man's eyes when he realizes once and for all that the woman he thinks he loves doesn't want his child. In an instant, his dreams of coaching Little League go down the tubes and...I don't care ever to see that look again."

Ben found this story hard to swallow. Why would Keely, who had so much to offer a child, decide not to have one? He couldn't imagine her being that selfish. Nora, his ex-wife, yes, but not Keely. But before he could object, she continued.

"I don't keep all men at arm's length," she said. "Just the ones I'm really attracted to. Just the ones in whom I see potential—potential for a serious relationship." She looked him right in the eye when she said it, almost as if she were issuing a threat.

A dozen objections to her ludicrous logic died on his lips. A moment ago he would have pointed out that not all men considered children the be-all and end-all. Take him, for instance. He was thirty-eight years old, with a daughter almost grown. Did she honestly think a man his age, one who had been to hell and back with one child, would want a *baby?*

But he was also a confirmed bachelor. His marriage had failed miserably, and while he'd like to blame Nora for everything, he knew many of their problems were as much his fault as hers. If Keely saw in him potential for a *serious* relationship—as in one ending up in matrimony—she would be sorely disappointed. He could predict only heartbreak up that road. She'd given him fair warning, and quite deliberately, too. He should consider himself lucky and get out fast and clean.

"I see," he said inanely.

"Good. Would you like to listen to some music?"

She had to be kidding. He couldn't possibly switch from such a personal conversation to the idle chitchat they'd enjoyed before. He needed to be alone. He needed to absorb everything she'd told him. "I think this might be a good time for me to cut out."

Again, he couldn't tell what the expression on her face meant. It could have been disappointment or relief.

"If you like," she said pleasantly. She stood, and he followed suit. "I've enjoyed the evening, despite its little ups and downs. You're very nice to talk to."

"So are you."

"And I hope you will call me when you're ready to talk about Tina. I still think family counseling would be good. Oh, and there's a parenting class coming up that might be helpful," she added as she walked him to the door. "Four sessions on Tuesday evenings, starting next week."

"I'll think about it." But he probably wouldn't.

Standing at her front door, he'd never felt so awkward in his life. "Ah, hell," he muttered. Then he leaned down and kissed her on the cheek before turning to leave.

Keely leaned against the doorframe, her hand lightly rubbing the cheek he'd just kissed, and unabashedly watched him walk to his car. "Well, you certainly scared *him* away, didn't you," she murmured to herself. Reluctantly she closed the door on the sight of his retreating Porsche, then slowly returned to the living room. She picked up the forgotten bottle of well-ventilated wine and poured herself a glass. She might as well enjoy it before it turned to vinegar.

Less than a mile away, Ben slowed his car to a crawl. He'd done the right thing, hadn't he? She'd looked so sad when she'd revealed those very personal facts to him, so vulnerable. Her decision must have caused her a great deal of pain in the past.

He'd felt the urge to hold her, comfort her, make everything all right for her. But of course it wasn't within his power to do that. She had *chosen* not to become a parent, and no one but Keely could change that. Nor was it in either of their best interests to encourage any further closeness.

But now, looking back, it seemed harsh that he'd just walked out on her. Her husband, and other men, too, had rejected her when she'd informed them of her wish to remain childless. He had immediately judged them insensitive bastards. Then he'd turned around and left.

Impulsively he turned on the next side street. He would go back. He would tell her he was sorry, and that he wanted to see her again. He wasn't like all those other jerks—he didn't want any more children. He and Keely were a perfect match! He would tell her...

He circled the block, then turned toward home. He wouldn't tell her anything until he'd thought this out. If he returned to her house in his current confused and hormone-driven state, he might say or do something that would hurt her even more in the long run. He might involve himself more deeply than he wanted to be, too.

When Ben arrived home, he was surprised to see Tina's Firebird parked in the driveway. She'd said she would be at a party tonight, a few blocks away.

The house was dark. Maybe one of her girlfriends had picked her up. Then he spotted the motorcycle parked at the curb.

Damn. It belonged to that Saxon kid. Of all the boys Tina had attracted, Todd Saxon was Ben's least favorite. As Ben entered the house, he took a deep breath and prepared himself for whatever surprise the teenagers had in store for him.

The stereo was turned up, so they didn't hear him until he was in the darkened living room. Then the two bodies enmeshed on the couch sprang apart as if they'd been doused with the garden hose.

Ben bit his lip. This could have been much worse—at least they both had their clothes on. Kissing was normal, acceptable behavior for a sixteen-year-old, although he wished she wouldn't do it in an empty house. Still, he wasn't going to lose his temper about it.

"Dad, what are you doing home so early?" Tina demanded, already on the defensive. "You came to check up on me, didn't you?"

"Did I need to check up on you?" he asked mildly as he reached to turn down the heavy-metal music.

"I thought you trusted me."

"I did—do," he said. "It just so happens that my date with Dr. . . ." He caught himself just in time. Tina would never forgive him if he revealed to Todd the identity of his date. "My date was cut short," he concluded.

Tina couldn't hide her smug pleasure over that announcement.

"I thought you were going to a party," Ben said irritably.

"We are. But it's barely nine o'clock. Dad, only geeks show up at a party before nine. C'mon, Todd, let's go." They both reached for the matching black leather jackets draped over the arm of the couch.

"Uh, just a minute, Tina," Ben said. "Could I speak to you in the kitchen?"

Tina rolled her eyes and looked as if she might balk, but in the end she followed her father through the louvered doors.

"You aren't going to tell me I can't go," she declared as soon as they were in private. She folded her arms mutinously.

"No. But why didn't you tell me you had a date?"

"It's not a date," she said hotly. "Todd stopped by to see if I was going to the party."

"Do you always make out with boys who just stop by?"

"Dad!" Despite her obvious irritation with him, Ben could tell she was embarrassed. "I like Todd, all right? Don't ruin everything."

"How old is he?"

She sighed elaborately. "He's a senior. He makes good grades and he's going to college, and he doesn't do drugs," she said all in a rush, "and just because he has kinda long hair and wears an earring—"

"Okay, okay," Ben relented. "Go to your party. But you drive your car. I don't want you riding on the back of his motorcycle under any circumstances."

"Dad..."

"Tina, I mean it. You know—"

"Yes, I know your best friend in high school was killed on a motorcycle. All right. We'll take my car."

Ben tried to lean down and give her a peck on the forehead, but she dodged him and made a quick, sullen exit.

He couldn't resist looking out the window as the teenagers departed. Tina dutifully climbed into the Firebird, while Todd took his motorcycle. Tina would probably park her car and hop on back of the bike the moment they were out of Ben's sight.

He shook his head. What was he going to do with her?

His thoughts drifted back to the parenting class Keely had mentioned. What was a "parenting" class, anyway? Since when had "parent" become a verb? Could something like that really help him?

Maybe he didn't need help. Maybe he was just experiencing the normal growing pains of watching a teenager assert her independence.

Sure. And maybe pigs could fly. As he mindlessly reached into the cookie jar for an Oreo, he decided to call the school on Monday and find out more about the class.

* * *

Keely rushed down the school hallway, the folder containing her class notes clutched to her chest. A car accident on the Paseo Bridge had delayed her a good ten minutes. She wasn't late, but she would be if she didn't hurry.

At least it wasn't a large class, she mused as she rounded a corner. The secretary had told her that nine parents were enrolled. With that few, she could use a less formal, more individualized approach.

She reached the classroom exactly one minute before seven. Out of breath, she greeted several women and one man, who stood talking in nervous little clutches. "I meant to be here earlier so I could greet you as you arrived, but the traffic...well, you don't want to hear about it. You probably get your fill of excuses from your kids."

Her bit of humor elicited a laugh and broke the ice, setting the right mood. She pushed aside the cumbersome lectern and perched on the edge of the table at the front of the room, then waited for the class members to find chairs.

"Let's introduce ourselves and then each of you can, if you like, bring up a problem you're having with your teenager. And if you aren't having any problems...I'll let you teach the class." That brought another laugh.

"I'll start. I'm Keely Adams. I don't have any children of my own..." After her recent bout of soul-searching, she found the words easier than usual to say. "But I've been counseling high school students for almost ten years. So while yours will eventually grow up into adults, I have to deal with a never-ending supply."

"What a nightmare," said one of the women with a laugh. "I'm Julia Sperry. My problem is my kid's grades. He won't study and he just doesn't seem to care."

One by one they all opened up to Keely, bringing up dilemmas large and small.

"... her new friends are a bunch of hoods!"

"... I think he might be using drugs."

"... found one of *those* magazines under his mattress."

"I'm worried about my daughter being promiscuous."

Keely inhaled sharply as her head swiveled toward the sound of that voice.

Ben Kinkaid loomed in the doorway. "Am I too late to join?" he asked.

Keely grasped for composure. "No, not at all," she replied, sounding a bit breathless. "I'm glad you could make it."

She meant that in several respects. For one thing, he needed this class. Tina was enough to challenge even the most savvy parent, and Ben had a lot to learn. But she was also just plain happy to see him. As she watched him make his way to the back of the classroom and select a desk, she couldn't deny the rush of pleasure she felt. He looked good in those faded jeans.

"We're going to discuss all of the problems you've brought brought up, and more, during the next four weeks," she began again. "First we're going to talk about why kids behave in ways that seem illogical to us. Understanding the reasons is the first step toward dealing effectively with them."

She passed out a syllabus, then began her lecture in earnest. She'd taught this class so many times that she hardly referred to her notes.

The moment she paused, questions came fast and furious—from everyone except Ben. He never raised his hand, and she resisted purposely drawing him into discussion. This wasn't a group therapy session, after all. But his wary gaze remained riveted on her, giving her not even a brief respite from his intent watchfulness.

Keely felt as if those green-gold eyes would melt her before the two-hour session was over. But when nine o'clock finally came, she was still miraculously walking on two solid legs and speaking coherently, despite the continuous pounding of her restless heart.

She handed out a list of books that the parents might find helpful. "I'll see you next week," she finished. Then she made a show of putting away her notes and erasing the chalkboard, giving Ben the opportunity to slip out without speaking to her. After the awkwardness of their last meeting, and then the way she'd practically driven him off with a stick, she didn't dream he would want to be alone with her. He was here because of Tina, period.

When the sounds of the departing parents faded into distant footfalls down the hall, Keely set down her eraser, turned back toward the empty classroom and gathered her things. She felt an undeniable pang of disappointment that she'd been right. Ben didn't want to talk.

As she straightened the desks and chairs, it occurred to her that she probably should have left with the others. Now she would have to walk through an empty school and into a deserted parking lot alone.

She turned out the light, stepped into the hall and locked the door behind her. With her folder again clutched against her chest and her car keys in hand, to be used as a weapon if necessary, she began walking down the long hall. She'd been mugged once during a walk to her car in a school parking lot. And although this was a different school in a much safer neighborhood, she was still alert to danger.

She exited through a steel double door, which locked behind her, and resumed her brisk, no-nonsense stride toward her car.

"Keely?"

She shrieked and dropped both her folder and her purse before the voice's familiarity reached her consciousness. "Oh, Ben, *damn,* you scared me," she said on a breathless laugh.

"Sorry about that." He bent to pick up the things she'd dropped. "I thought you saw me."

"No. I was so intent on spotting the muggers and such, I guess I missed a perfectly innocent person staring me right in the face."

"I wouldn't say 'innocent,'" he drawled as he returned her folder and her purse.

His hands brushed hers, not on purpose. But instantly she remembered what those hands felt like flattened against her back, or sifting through her short hair. She shivered and told herself it was the brisk evening breeze.

"Let's go get some coffee at Papa Joe's," he suggested.

She nodded. "This isn't a chance meeting, I take it?" she ventured as they made their way toward his gleaming sports car.

"No. I deliberately stalked you." He laughed evily.

"Wouldn't it have been simpler just to come talk to me after class?"

They paused at the passenger door, and he grew very serious. "I intended to. But you looked like maybe you didn't want anything to do with me, and I chickened out."

"And then discovered your courage in the parking lot."

"I tried to get back in, but the door had locked." With that he let her into the car. It smelled like fine leather and, very faintly, of Ben. Keely breathed deeply of the intoxicating blend of fragrances as she fastened her seat belt.

Ben climbed in a moment later and started the powerful engine. Neither of them spoke until they'd reached Papa Joe's, an all-night pancake house that featured iridescent booths, mean-tempered waitresses and the best coffee north of the Missouri River.

Finally, when they were seated on opposite sides of a booth with steaming mugs in front of them, Ben cleared his throat. "I'm sorry I ran out on you Saturday night. That was a lousy thing to do."

"I understand why you did," Keely countered, though she didn't refute his claim that it was lousy. "I laid some pretty heavy stuff on you."

"I pushed you into it. And no, I don't think you understand at all." His steady gaze was fixed on her, so intense that she felt like a butterfly pinned to a board.

She didn't dare argue. Instead she busied her hands by ripping open a packet of sugar and dumping it into her cup. She didn't even like sugar in coffee.

"Keely, I don't give a damn that you don't want babies."

Her hands froze, and the empty sugar packet floated into her cup unheeded. "What?"

"I mean, the fact of the matter is, I'm almost forty years old. What would I do with a baby? I've got enough problems with the child I already have."

Keely used her spoon to fish the paper out of her coffee. Here she was, discussing having babies with a man she really didn't know all that well, and it was her own hysteria that had brought her to this, her overblown insecurities. She took a sip of the coffee and steeled herself for what she had to say.

"Ben, I'm glad you brought this up, because I probably wouldn't have been brave enough to start this conversation on my own. But since you did..." She took another gulp of coffee. "After you left Saturday night, I drank about half that bottle of wine, got just a little tipsy and did some hard thinking. And I realized something. It's been ten years since I decided to rule out man/woman relationships from my life. At the time my reasons seemed valid. But now...well, people in our age bracket aren't necessarily interested in starting a family.''

"That's what I just said.''

"Yes, but that's only part of what I realized. I think that, just *maybe*, I've been hiding behind this no-baby excuse. It does make a handy shield. I don't have to get involved with anyone, and if I do, and they reject me, I can always blame it on the fact that I'm...that I refuse to have children. Then I don't have to face the uncomfortable possibility that I might not be ultimately lovable and perfect in every other respect.''

Ben gave a low whistle. "Aren't you being a little hard on yourself, Dr. Adams?''

She gave a self-deprecating smile. "Professional hazard. We psychologists either ignore our own problems completely, or analyze ourselves to death.''

Ben absently stirred his coffee. When he spoke again, it was with deceptive casualness. "Does this mean I can kiss you?''

Her heart did a somersault, but she nodded almost imperceptibly. She hoped he would do more than kiss her. It was high time for Keely Adams to come out of the cloister.

Four

Ben's pulse raced crazily as he paid for their coffee. The challenge had been issued and accepted. There would be no backing down now. He had committed himself to kissing Keely. And kissing her would never be enough.

Accepting his change from the cashier, he chanced a sideways glance at Keely. She looked at least as apprehensive as he felt, with a vivid blush coloring her cheeks. She ran nervous fingers through her shiny cap of hair, then shot him a tentative smile.

This was new, exciting territory for both of them.

Suddenly it seemed vital that their first kiss—their first *important* kiss, he amended—be just right. He wanted to let her know how much he desired her, yet he didn't want to overwhelm her.

They walked to his car without touching, but the anticipation was an almost palpable thing between them.

"Looks like rain," Keely said, peering up at the halos of mist surrounding the parking lot's floodlights.

Ben nodded his agreement. He could smell the dampness in the air. "It's cooler, too," he said as he hunched his shoulders inside his windbreaker. Keely wore only a thin sweater. He hurried to let her into the shelter of his car.

When they were both settled, he started the engine and the heater, but he made no move to put the car in gear. He looked at her. She looked at him. Then they both started laughing.

"Shall we talk about the weather some more?" he asked.

She laughed again, a sweet, melodic sound. She looked fresh-faced and full of life, like an innocent girl on her first date.

He didn't feel at all innocent.

"Are we acting as silly as I think we are?" she asked. "After all this dramatic buildup, aren't you afraid the actual kiss will be anticlimactic?"

"Not likely," he said with an emphatic shake of his head and a wicked smile. He had no doubts that when he kissed her, it would be even better than he remembered.

He recalled what he'd said to Tina the week before, about teenagers and parking and scoring in the back seat. He'd been kidding then, but... He glanced over his shoulder at the Porsche's minuscule back seat, then shook his head at his own foolishness. Hormones made men— and women, he supposed—do strange things.

He put the car in gear and headed out into the street, perfectly aware that Keely was watching him intently. It took only a couple of minutes to reach the school parking lot. It was raining now. He pulled up so that his passenger door was adjacent to her driver's door.

"I...thank you for the coffee," she said, looking down.

He reached up and touched her cheek with a feathery caress, then ran his finger from her shoulder down her arm to her hand. He grasped her hand firmly and brought it to his lips. Her skin was cool and smooth and smelled faintly of hand lotion.

Her eyebrows slowly rose. "That's it?"

"Oh, no, that's not it. That's just a small sample of what's to come. Can I take you to dinner Friday night?"

Keely understood. He didn't want to kiss her in the front seat of a car in a school parking lot. Frankly, she didn't much care where he kissed her, as long as he got on with it. The anticipation was killing her. He knew it, too, and she got the distinct impression he enjoyed making her wait.

"Friday, yes, I'd like that," she said, at last responding to his invitation.

"Good. I'll pick you up at seven. Oh, there's something you should know. Tina won't like this."

Ah, yes, Tina. Keely was ashamed that she had all but forgotten the girl in her preoccupation with her father. "She's still afraid we're conspiring against her?"

"It's more than that. Tina is used to having me to herself. She gets jealous when I date. In fact, she told me I was too old to date."

Keely rolled her eyes. "Teenagers are so tactful."

"You have a good relationship with her," Ben continued. "You've made a positive impact on her. I don't want to undermine that."

"Neither do I. But it's not a good idea to let her dictate your social life, either. She needs to understand that our seeing each other and my counseling her are two separate, distinct things. So if she makes a fuss, just reassure her that we won't violate her privacy. Discussions about Tina will be reserved for parenting classes and counseling sessions."

Ben shook his head. "She still won't like it."

"She may not like it, but she'll have to learn that the world doesn't always cater to her whims. It might be a good lesson." She smiled reassuringly. Ben's concern for Tina was one of the most endearing things about him. A lot of men didn't care what their children thought of their dates.

He smiled back, although it was a shaky attempt at best. "Till Friday, then. Wear something dressy." He squeezed her hand and released it in a perfectly gentlemanly fashion, but the way he looked at her was pure rogue. The dancing light in his green-gold eyes warmed her from the inside out and kept her warm during the long, wet drive home.

Tina was standing in the living room, arms folded, foot tapping, when Ben arrived home. She looked pointedly at her watch. "Where have you been?"

Ben was taken aback by the demand. Suddenly they'd reversed roles. Tina was the irate parent and he the teenager, home late from a date. "I told you, I went to that parenting class."

"For three and a half hours? Right, I'm supposed to believe that."

He felt like telling her it was none of her damn business what he did with his time, but he bit his tongue. "Keely and I went for coffee afterward," he said as he slipped out of his windbreaker and hung it in the coat closet.

"Then you admit it?"

He looked at his daughter, bewildered by the vehemence he saw in her face. He'd expected disapproval, but not so strong. "I admit that I asked her to have coffee so I could talk to her alone. I hope to be seeing more of her. I'm not trying to hide anything."

"Then it's true. This 'concerned father' routine is just a way for you to get into Dr. Adams's—"

"Tina Ann Kinkaid, if you finish that sentence you can plan on spending the next month in your room," Ben bellowed. "I will not have you speak with such disrespect about anyone, least of all Keely Adams."

Tina stared down at her bare feet and bit her lower lip.

"Is that clear?"

She nodded, then snuffled. Damn, he'd made her cry. He could count on one hand the number of times he had yelled at her that way. She always cried ... or was she acting? In the parenting class, Keely had discussed the many ways teenagers manipulate their parents. Tina wasn't above a few dramatics.

Ah, hell, he might as well hang it up. Real or feigned, nothing undid him like a little girl's tears. Or a woman's tears, he reminded himself. Tina was hardly a little girl.

He took her by the shoulders and gently guided her to the sofa. She sat down without protest, and he sat next to her.

"I'm sorry I yelled at you, sweetheart, but face it, sometimes you deserve it. It's over, now. I'm not mad at you."

She nodded again, her silver earrings making a tinkling sound.

Ben flicked one of the earrings with his finger. "These are pretty. Are they new?"

"Todd gave them to me."

Todd. Ben gritted his teeth and forced himself to come up with a pleasant rejoinder. If he expected Tina to accept Keely, he would have to set a good example by accepting Tina's choice in boyfriends. "Sounds pretty serious."

"It's not. He's okay. Daddy, I don't want to talk about Todd."

"Okay, then let's talk about me and Dr. Adams. If you would think about it, we never would have met in the first place if she hadn't been concerned about you. As for me— yes, I liked Keely from the moment I met her. But even if she'd been an ogre, married with thirteen kids, I still would have gone to her for help and advice because I want to do what's best for you. You'll always be my first priority."

"But you're still gonna go out with her."

"Yes. I'm taking her out Friday night."

"Daddy—"

"And before you even say it, no, we won't plot against you." He struggled to remember exactly what Keely had said to tell Tina. "The fact that she's counseling you has nothing to do with our seeing each other on a social basis. We won't discuss you outside of the parenting class, and you know she'll always respect your privacy."

Tina slumped against the back of the couch and folded her arms. "I still don't like it."

"But you'll have to live with it. I hope you'll do it gracefully... like the mature adult you're growing into."

Ben knew he'd gone too far with that last bit when Tina grimaced and performed a dramatic pantomime of gagging. "Oh puh-leeze, Daddy." With that she bolted from the sofa and stomped away to her basement bedroom, slamming the door behind her.

Keely had told him to be firm with Tina, but every time he was, she got angry. It was so tempting to give in to his daughter's wishes and restore harmony. But this was not the time to allow Tina to manipulate him. This chance with Keely—the first woman to interest him in a very long time—was too important.

Keely studied herself critically in the bathroom mirror. Other than a couple of outdated bridesmaids' dresses, she

owned nothing fancy, so she'd borrowed this outfit from
one of the secretaries. The sky blue silk sheath featured a
sensible neckline and modest cap sleeves. But beyond that,
all claim to conservatism had been abandoned. The shim-
mering silk clung to her curves like a second skin. The hem
reached almost to her knees, but a daring slit up the side
revealed quite a bit of thigh with her every step.

She didn't look quite like herself. But for tonight, perhaps it wouldn't hurt to be someone other than conserva-
tive, boring Keely Adams. After all, how often did a
dangerously gorgeous man take her out for an expensive
dinner and threaten her with kisses?

She grew light-headed at the thought of those kisses. Did
he have any idea what he'd done to her, making her wait
three whole days? She was consumed with the thought of
how his arms would feel around her, his mouth hot and
demanding against hers, his tongue . . .

Her eyes snapped open. That was the doorbell, and here
she was with her cheeks burning a too-healthy pink. She
tried a confident smile. Not bad, considering she was
about to embark on her first real date in years. Hopefully,
no one, including Ben, would know she was scared to
death.

The sight of him standing on her front porch literally
took her breath away. Even in a dignified gray suit, he
broadcast an aura of pure ruggedness. His golden tan
against the crisp white shirt spoke of countless afternoons
outdoors, and his light brown hair was already springing
free of the style he'd combed it into, returning to its naturally unruly waves.

But the untamed look in his leonine eyes was what most
captivated her. As she took him in, he practially devoured
her with his hot gaze.

"Wow," he finally said.

That single word, packed with so much feeling, was enough to maintain her blush for hours to come, she was sure. "Come on in," she said, knowing she wore a silly grin. "I think I'll need a wrap, don't you?"

"I'll keep you warm."

"Ben!"

"Sorry," he said, not sounding at all sorry as he closed the door. "Here, this is for you."

When Keely opened the white box he handed her, she stared mutely at the contents for several seconds.

"Uh-oh," Ben said. "Tina warned me I was hopelessly old-fashioned. She said you would think I was a geek."

"Oh, no, she's wrong. It's beautiful." She gingerly pulled the white orchid from the box, admiring it from every angle. "It's beautiful," she said again. "I've never had an orchid before." She extended it toward him. "Do you want to pin it on?"

This was a complication he hadn't counted on. He hadn't pinned a flower on a girl since high school, and even then he hadn't been good at it. Still, he gamely took a step closer to Keely, intending to give it his best shot. He had to slip his fingers beneath the neckline of her dress so that he didn't stab her with the pin. But once he touched her, he found it nearly impossible to apply himself to the task.

A subtle floral fragrance surrounded him—from the orchid? No, it was Keely's own intoxicating scent, impairing his senses. Her skin was velvety smooth where his fingers rubbed against it. His hands shook.

He ended up jabbing his thumb. The pin dropped. The corsage dropped. And somehow or another Keely was in his arms and he was kissing the living daylights out of her.

She was an incredibly warm, soft package of pure womanhood pressed against him. Her mouth received his eagerly; her tongue met his playfully. She gripped his hair

with one hand while the other slipped beneath his suit
jacket to splay against his ribs.

The feel of her, the smell of her, the taste of her was
enough to drive any man past reason. He let his hand slide
past the small of her back to the sweet curve of her hips,
pulling her more tightly against him. He didn't merely desire her. He wanted to crawl inside her skin.

It might have been a minute or several minutes later that
Keely pulled her mouth away from his. She looked at Ben
with dazed eyes, inky blue with arrested passion. But those
wide eyes also reflected confusion, anxiety and maybe even
a little fear.

That was enough to haul Ben back to his senses. Acute
desire did not give him the right to behave like a barbarian. Slowly he released her, taking a step back, carefully
straightening her pretty dress, smoothing a strand of hair
off her forehead.

"I'm sorry, Keely," he said, his voice heavy with the
wanting he couldn't quite suppress.

"Don't be." Still, she put even more distance between
them, backing into the breakfast bar that separated the
kitchen and dining room. She eased all the way around it,
until she was in one room and he in the other, with the bar
between them. "It wasn't entirely your fault. You had an
accomplice."

"But I frightened you."

"No," she said quickly, her gaze still locked with his. "I
frightened myself. It was so…" She paused, then changed
course. "It's been so long since I felt this way. You must
think I'm one of those stereotypical sex-starved old-maid
schoolteachers."

He smiled at the ridiculous image. "Hardly. I was too
worried about my own sex-starved state to pay much attention to yours." He reached across the bar and laid his

hand gently over hers. "You look sexy as hell, but I promise not to gobble you up. You don't have to stand in another room."

She looked around, as if only then aware that she had migrated. "Oh, I, uh, came in here to get a glass of water. Would you like one?"

A bucket of ice water, maybe, to dump over his head. "No, thanks."

She busied herself with getting a glass from the cabinet, ice cubes from the freezer, distilled water from a jug in the refrigerator. It gave them both a chance to compose themselves. After she took a long drink of the water, she turned toward him with a much calmer expression.

"I need to go slow with this," she said.

"Yes, I understand."

"I'm out of practice."

"Me, too. My control is rusty, that's for sure. Then again, I can't remember ever being treated to such a temptation." He couldn't help the way he looked at her. His hunger must have shown on his face, because Keely gave him a sloe-eyed look of her own. At least she wasn't afraid.

"Are you ready for dinner?" he asked, forcing himself to return to the real world. "I made reservations at Florentine's, but we could go somewhere else if you want."

"Oh, by all means, let's go to Florentine's. I've never been there. I peeked in the door once, and it smelled heavenly."

The tension between them eased. Ben felt more in control now. He bent to retrieve the orchid and pin, and he handed them to Keely as she joined him a minute later, carrying a white lace wrap of some sort over her arm. "Maybe you should put this on yourself," he said.

"Good idea." She made quick work of the corsage, then smiled sweetly as he held open the front door.

Given the way the evening had started, Ben was surprised that dinner turned out to be so easy and relaxed. At their quiet, candlelit table they shared rack of lamb for two while trading reminiscences of childhood. He learned that Keely's parents, both retired schoolteachers, still lived in the small town of Desmond, Missouri, where Keely had grown up. Her older sister, Eileen, had a husband, three rambunctious sons, and a farm not twenty miles from her hometown. Although Keely had bucked tradition to brave life in the big city, from the way she talked Ben could tell her family was still a close-knit one.

He was an only child, he told her, but he had numerous cousins who were almost like siblings. He had migrated from St. Louis to Kansas City to start a branch of his father's pool business.

"For Tina's sake, sometimes I wished I hadn't moved away," he confessed. "She adores her grandmother, but they don't see each other as often as they used to."

"An extended family close by can be good and bad," Keely said. "The support is wonderful, but relatives can interfere and cause friction, too. Oh, for heaven's sake, I'm sounding like a psychologist. Stop me before I analyze again."

"Would a slice of double-fudge truffle cake distract you from psychology?"

She groaned. "Normally you could talk me into chocolate anything. But I'm stuffed."

"Me, too. Let's split one."

They did. There was something delightfully intimate about sharing the rich dessert. The taste of it was almost sinful. Even more satisfying was watching Keely as she closed her eyes while a mouthful of the decadent stuff melted in her mouth. Someday soon, she was going to look that way when he made love to her.

He wouldn't rush her, though. He would wait until she was ready—till they were both ready. She was worth waiting for.

"You're a little late," Keely said as Tina banged the office door behind her on Wednesday of the following week. "Did something hold you up?" She was careful not to accuse.

Tina's expression was even more sullen than usual. It was to be expected. Ben had warned Keely that his daughter wasn't happy with the status quo.

"I was talking to Mr. Showalter," Tina said, making no move to put her books down or find a chair.

"Oh? Is it something you want to tell me?"

"Yeah. I told him I wanted to change counselors."

It took a moment for that to sink in. Keely had expected trouble from Tina, but she'd never imagined that the girl would take such drastic action.

It hurt. Anger and resentment she could handle, because she knew there was always a way around those emotions, if she worked hard enough. But for one of her students to reject her... well, it just didn't happen very often.

Keely somehow managed to hide her pain. "What did Mr. Showalter say?"

"He said he would talk to you and Dr. Penworth about it, but that it'd probably be okay."

John Penworth was the other psychological counselor at Graham. Generally the boys saw him and the girls preferred Keely, but there were some exceptions.

"Meanwhile, though," Tina continued, "I have to keep my appointment with you."

"It *is* part of your agreement," Keely said. "Why don't you sit down? Since this might be our last session, we ought to clean up any loose ends so you and Dr. Penworth can start more or less fresh.''

Tina stared at her suspiciously. Apparently she hadn't expected Keely to acquiesce so easily. She dropped her books onto the floor and sprawled on the couch.

"If you feel Dr. Penworth will be more help than me, I'll respect that decision. But I remember you once told me you would feel uncomfortable confiding in a man.''

"He might be a man, but at least he doesn't have the hots for my father.''

Keely ignored the crude expression and concentrated on the emotions behind it. "So you're changing counselors because your father and I went out on a date.''

"What did you think?''

"I figured that was it, but I wanted to be sure. Tina, the fact that your father and I are going out—''

"I've already heard that speech. Your dating has nothing to do with you counseling me, and you won't discuss me and you'll respect my privacy and all that junk.''

"You sound like you don't believe that.''

Tina rolled her eyes. "Forgive me, but, no way. If I came in here and told you I was pregnant or on drugs, you'd run to my father so fast—''

"No, I wouldn't,'' Keely insisted, rising from her chair in her agitation. "I would never do that. That would be unethical. I would never betray you or my profession that way.''

"Then why did my dad suddenly decide to grill me about birth control?'' Tina shot back.

Keely sank into her chair, frowning.

"So you *did* tell him,'' Tina concluded.

"No. No, I was just trying to remember what was said that first night when I came over to your house. At first I told him only the facts of the knife incident, and I told him what you told Mr. Showalter—that you thought you needed the knife for protection. Your father brought up the subject of your boyfriends. He was positive that you hadn't had sex with any of them and that you wouldn't.''

"And then you told him he was wrong."

"I told him that given the statistics, and the peer pressure, that he shouldn't dismiss the possibility quite so easily."

"Well, thanks a heap. Now he thinks I'm a slut. And you wonder why I want to change counselors? For your information, I haven't slept with anybody."

She wasn't lying. Keely'd had enough experience with teenage girls, and this teenage girl in particular, to know when they were telling a painful truth. For some reason this was a very touchy subject for Tina, and she looked about as hurt and vulnerable as a girl could get.

It took all of Keely's professional control not to take Tina into her arms and comfort her. Instead she sat on her hands, trying to decide how best to approach this newest problem. "I'm sorry," she said. It was a start.

Tina looked at her skeptically. "For what?"

"For assuming the wrong thing about you. For causing friction between you and your father. It's the last thing I wanted."

"Yeah? Well, it's all you've done ever since that first night you came to the house. Dad's been all over me."

"If your dad's been giving you a hard time, it's because he's trying to be a better parent. And, yes, I probably have something to do with that. But you seem to think that because we went out to dinner I'm giving him after-hours tutoring on how to make your life miserable, and that's just not true. We like each other. We enjoy each other's company—"

"I don't want to hear this."

"—and we don't discuss you at any great length."

"How can you say that?" Tina exploded. "I'm supposed to believe that when you're with me you're my counselor, and on Tuesday nights you're just a teacher and my dad is like any other parent, and when you go out with him you're just a girl and he's a guy? Come on, Dr. Adams, you would have to have split personalities to keep all that separate."

Keely sighed. She had been sure that there was no conflict of interest, but the way Tina had just presented the situation... At the very least, Tina no longer felt safe confiding in Keely. And Keely couldn't continue to provide effective counseling if her relationship with Ben created this much anxiety.

"Perhaps you're right," she said quietly. "If you really think you would be more comfortable with Dr. Penworth, then that's who your counselor should be. I'll meet with him in the next couple of days, then you and he can arrange your first appointment for later in the week. How's that?"

Tina nodded, looking visibly relieved. Then this wasn't just an emotional blackmail trick to drive Ben and Keely apart. The girl was in genuine distress.

"I'll miss you," Keely said, and she meant it. Tina had been a constant challenge, and yet something of a success story. "We've come a long way since our first session."

"Mmm." Tina grunted noncommittally.

"You can still talk to me anytime...as a friend."

"Yeah, right."

Keely wondered then—was it she in particular Tina didn't want dating her father, or would she resent any woman? Ben had indicated there had been problems in the past. Was the girl simply jealous that her doting father was paying attention to another female, or was there more to it?

"We have a few minutes left," Keely said. "Is there anything else you want to talk about?"

"No." Tina gathered her books, preparing to leave, then stopped and stared intently at Keely. "Yes. If I tell you it's okay to tell my dad something, can you do that? I wouldn't want you to compromise your precious ethics."

"If you give me permission, yes."

"Then tell him I don't sleep around. Some of my friends do, *all* of the boys do, but I don't. I may not be the most popular girl in the sophomore class, but I don't plan to turn out like my mother." On the heels of that impassioned speech, she turned and left Keely staring openmouthed.

Five

"**Y**ou look simply divine, my dear," Ben said with a courtly bow as Keely tried on a moth-eaten velvet hat sporting a wilted sprig of silk flowers.

"No better than you, sir," she said, nodding toward the six-inch-wide tie around his neck, which featured psychedelic hula girls. They had decided to spend that Saturday roaming the antique shops in nearby St. Joseph, having discovered a mutual passion for unusual objets d'art and downright weird things.

Ben hunted for a reasonably priced mantel clock, while Keely peered into every nook and cranny for egg cups to add to her collection. Neither of them found what they were looking for, but they discovered a lot of other strange and wonderful things and soon had the trunk of Ben's car stuffed full.

Hot and dusty after more than two hours of treasure-hunting, they stopped for a late lunch at an old-fashioned café. It was then, over hamburgers and lemonade, that Keely broached the subject she'd been avoiding.

"I hope you don't mind if I slip into the role of counselor for a few minutes, but I need to talk to you about Tina."

A wariness came over Ben's features. "I thought that subject was taboo."

"Not in this case. I'm allowed to tell you that she changed counselors."

Ben's eyes widened in surprise, then narrowed. Apparently he hadn't known.

"She's seeing John Penworth now."

"Not if I have anything to say about it. You've done more for her than anyone else, including me. How can she even think..." He cut himself off. "Never mind. I'll straighten it out."

"Ben, I think this time we should let it go. If I thought she was simply being obstinate for obstinacy's sake, I would fight to keep her as my client. But she's not. She feels betrayed."

"That's ridiculous," Ben scoffed. "She knows we both want the best for her. How have we betrayed her?"

"It has to do with trust. My office used to be a safe haven for her. She could complain about her teachers, her friends—"

"And me," Ben added.

"And you, secure because the worst that could happen would be that I would urge her to think things through, or look at them from a different perspective. I was nonthreatening. But things changed when I took a more active role by confronting you and trying to save her from being expelled. I managed to keep her in school, but by taking things outside my office I lost her trust."

"And by getting to know me."

"That's certainly part of it." Keely sighed, feeling unreasonably sad. "Penworth is good. He'll keep her on course."

Ben chewed on his straw, a thoughtful expression on his face. "Do you think we made a mistake?"

Keely shrugged uncomfortably. "Tina *was* playing us against each other for sympathy. By coming to see you I forced her to be more honest with both of us, and there's nothing wrong with that. Also, you needed some parenting advice."

"No kidding."

"But I had no idea things would happen so fast, that you and I would . . . well, I rationalized it a hundred different ways. But when it comes right down to it, I should have known better. I should have kept things on a professional level."

"I wasn't going to let you do that," Ben pointed out. After a pause, he added, "Keely, would it help if we . . ."

"Broke things off?" she supplied.

"Uh-huh," he said without much enthusiasm. "Don't get me wrong. I don't *want* to stop seeing you. I haven't enjoyed a woman's company like this in a long, long time. But if I'm doing wrong by my daughter . . ."

Keely nodded her understanding. "The thought *has* crossed my mind. But—and I hope this isn't my selfishness talking—I think it's too late to backtrack. I've lost Tina's trust, and once that's gone, it's damned impossible to get it back. My feeling is that we should go on about our business, and hope that Dr. Penworth can help Tina work through her resentment."

"I was hoping you'd say something like that." Ben reached across the table and squeezed her hand, an unmistakably possessive gesture that sent shivers all the way to her toes. "I don't want to stop seeing you, Keely."

She squeezed back, touched by the earnestness she saw in his green-gold eyes but shaken a bit by the hunger. A similar craving burned somewhere deep inside her. Whether or not she was ready, someday soon their mutual desires would explode, catapulting them into uncharted, risky territory.

"Oh, there's something else," she said before she could get carried away with her thoughts and forget her responsibility to Tina.

"More?" Ben frowned, although he continued to hold Keely's hand, rubbing his thumb absently over her knuckles.

"Tina specifically asked me to inform you that she hasn't 'slept around.'"

Ben groaned. "That's what I get for trying to be open. I innocently asked her if she had all the information she needed in the way of birth control, if she wanted to see a doctor or anything, and she took it as an accusation. Nearly bit my head off."

"My mistake again. I shouldn't have alarmed you."

"Then you think she's telling the truth?" he asked hopefully.

"I really do. She was so adamant about it. She said she didn't want to turn out... like her mother."

Ben's jaw dropped in surprise before he quickly snapped it closed. Then he leaned back in his chair, releasing Keely's hand. "I didn't realize she *knew* that about her mother. She was only seven when we divorced, and she's never heard anything about Nora's affairs from me. How could she have figured out...."

"Children observe more than we think, sometimes."

Ben shook his head. "Nora hasn't shown her face in almost ten years. We hardly mention her in passing anymore. Why would Tina suddenly bring this up?"

"Probably because she's growing up, and it's time for her to deal with her mother's desertion on a more adult level." Keely could have added that Tina was feeling overwhelmed by the onset of her own sexuality—that she really might be afraid of turning out like her mother—but that was probably more than Ben wanted to hear.

"Should I talk to her about it?" he asked. "Never mind. I forgot, she's not your responsibility anymore."

Keely frowned at the reminder.

"It wouldn't surprise me if Tina were bitter," Ben said, almost as if he were thinking aloud. "Nora was a terrible mother. She resented Tina, resented me for getting her pregnant and never made a secret of the fact."

Keely couldn't think of any way to respond to those harsh words, so she simply laid her hand on his arm.

He smiled wanly. "Then again, I don't suppose I'm the world's best father. I'm not exactly batting a thousand."

She struggled to find something comforting to say. "No parent makes the smartest decisions every time. But you're not doing too badly. You love Tina, and that's what matters."

"You're the one who made the smart decision."

She looked at him quizzically.

"You chose not to have kids. Sometimes I wish . . ."

Keely's response was swift and emphatic. "No, you don't, Ben. Don't ever say that."

He sat up straight and studied her. "I wasn't serious. You know I wouldn't trade Tina for anything. But I'll tell you something. I would never have another child. I wouldn't go through this again, not in a million years."

She longed to tell him how very lucky he was, how even a difficult child was a far cry better than no child at all. But she kept her own counsel. If things continued as they were, if she and Ben grew closer, maybe she would be able to reveal the facts of her infertility. At least then he would understand that she *wanted* children, unlike Nora. But she had guarded the secret for so long that confiding in him wouldn't be easy.

At least she'd come this far. She was dating again, slowly allowing herself to feel the physical yearnings she had denied herself, the emotions she'd once shut away. Maybe there was hope for her yet.

"Please, Daddy? You said if I passed all my classes and didn't make any D's I could have a reward."

Ben looked up distractedly from the shrub he was trimming. Tina was in the swimming pool, propped on her elbows and leaning over the concrete edge. "Your report card isn't even here yet."

"Daddy, you're not paying attention. I know what I'm getting in every class. A's, B's and only two C's. You said I could have a reward. Can I please go to the lake? The Paleys have a big boat and water skis and inner tubes, and everyone else is going."

"Are Mr. and Mrs. Paley going to be there?"

"You don't think they would turn their house over to a bunch of kids if they weren't, do you?"

It didn't escape Ben that Tina hadn't directly answered the question. But he decided not to pursue it. Things had been going so smoothly over the past three weeks that he hated to rock the boat. Tina's grades were excellent. She'd received a raise at work. And her attitude toward Keely had softened considerably.

"And you'll be spending the night?"

"Just the girls are sleeping over. The boys will go home tonight and come back tomorrow."

Right. He'd like to see all those hormone-infested boys calmly heading for home at the end of the day. Still, maybe

it was time for him to trust Tina again, although every time
he did he got a kick in the teeth.

"I guess you can go, if you promise to—"

"Thank you, thank you, thank you, Daddy." Tina
sprang out of the pool like a cork from a champagne bottle and gave him a wet hug. "Todd's picking me up in less
than half an hour. I have to get packed!"

Todd again. Ben sighed. "Pretty sure of yourself, aren't
you."

"I thought you would say yes in the end," she confessed with an impish smile. Then her expression darkened. "I suppose you'll be seeing Keely tonight." Her voice
dripped with disapproval. She had softened—she wasn't
throwing screaming fits anymore. But she was far from
accepting of her father's social life.

"I'd planned on having her over for dinner."

"And I suppose, since you'll have the house to yourself, that she'll be spending the night?"

"That's none of your business," he said through gritted teeth even as his blood surged at the picture his
daughter had painted.

"Why not?"

"Because certain things should be private between two
people."

Tina eyes him speculatively. "Are you sure about that?"

"Yes, of course! What are you driving at?"

"Nothing," she said innocently as she grabbed her towel
from a deck chair. She turned and hurried toward the
house, calling over her shoulder, "I'll be back tomorrow
night!"

Ben refused to let his daughter's cryptic comments
bother him for long. They probably meant nothing. Tina
was always saying provocative things. At any rate, he had

his own dilemmas to worry about—such as whether he *would* ask Keely to spend the night.

They had seen each other two or three times a week for over a month now. Each time he kissed her good-night, it was more difficult to walk away. Her softly scented skin, the warm response of her mouth against his, the raw need he sometimes saw in her fathomless blue eyes—these plagued his fantasies by day and wove through his dreams at night.

If ever there was a time to allow themselves deeper intimacy, this was it. They had nothing more strenuous planned than to swim, fix a little dinner and listen to music. With Tina safely occupied miles away, they wouldn't have to deal with the added pressure of her disapproval.

But was Keely ready? She hadn't been able to disguise the fire inside that sometimes threatened to rage out of control. Her emotions were a different story. Trusting him with her fragile feelings couldn't be easy, not after the raw deals she'd gotten from her ex-husband and those other bozos she'd dated.

He couldn't imagine why a man would…then again, as a young man he might have thought twice about a serious involvement with a woman who didn't want children. She was entitled to that position, of course, but as a man who'd once been committed to the idea of raising a brood of his own…

Ah, hell, it was a moot point. He wasn't a young man anymore, he didn't want more children and that made him and Keely perfectly suited. Even the idea of a *serious* relationship didn't scare him anymore, not with her.

When she showed up later that afternoon, Ben dismissed his worries and concentrated on enjoying the evening—an especially easy task, since it involved watching Keely swim in a sleek, green swimsuit.

The one-piece suit was sexier than any bikini could have been, he decided as she displayed her small repertoire of underwater acrobatics for him. She came to the surface after a somersault with the thin nylon clinging to every curve of her well-toned body. He could see the slight indentation of her navel, count her ribs and watch with interest every time the cool breeze hit her wet body, causing her nipples to crest into hard peaks.

He thought of slipping the strap down her shoulder, freeing her breast and bending to take that hard pebble into his mouth.

She saw the direction of his gaze. As if reading his thoughts, she gave him an admonishing look—though not too stern. "Want to see a handstand?" she asked. Without waiting for his reply, she plunged below the surface. Moments later her long, slender legs popped up, pointing gracefully toward the sky. Her suit did little to hide the intriguing curves of her derriere.

His mouth went dry.

She came up for air, laughing. It was gratifying to see her relaxed and happy around him—nothing at all like that night she had grilled hamburgers on her deck.

"That's about the extent of my water ballet," she said, shaking the water out of one ear. "What tricks can you do?"

He wasn't going to touch that one. "I may build pools, but I leave the strenuous swimming to my customers. My forte is floating around on a raft."

"And catching rays," she added. She reached toward him, as if she was going to touch his chest, then seemed to think better of it. "You were tan even back in April, when we first met."

"That's from working outdoors year-round."

Another breeze blew over them, and Keely shivered.

"Cold?"

She nodded. "Getting waterlogged, too. Not to mention hungry."

"You can shower and change in the bathroom at the top of the stairs," he said as they waded toward the pool steps. "I'll fire up the grill."

Keely rinsed off quickly, towel-dried her hair, then threw on the white shorts and striped cotton top she'd brought with her. She felt good tonight—better than she had in weeks, months, perhaps even years. She had the energy of a puppy, the appetite of a horse and a smile that wouldn't quit.

All because of Ben Kinkaid.

Her libido was plenty revved up, too, and unless she missed her guess, Ben knew it. How could he miss it, when she looked at him with all the subtlety of a lioness eyeing an antelope buck? She might as well have been wearing a neon sign advertising her readiness. She had all but cheered when Ben had casually mentioned that Tina was out of the house until tomorrow evening.

She applied a touch of mascara and a quick swipe of lip gloss before rejoining Ben downstairs in the kitchen.

He had changed, too, into well-worn jeans and a long-sleeved T-shirt that bore his company logo. He smiled when he looked up and saw her. She liked the way his eyes crinkled at the edges.

"What can I do to help?" she asked.

"You can build yourself a couple of shish kebabs." He nodded toward the makings laid out on the kitchen island. "Meanwhile, do you like frozen Margaritas?"

"Mmm, love 'em." She shamelessly filled two skewers to capacity, stacked heavily in favor of mushrooms, then put on a pot of quick rice as Ben took the kebabs outside and set them to sizzle on the grill. That done, she sat down at the umbrella table on the patio and sipped her icy drink, enjoying the mouth-watering aroma of marinated beef and tangy vegetables.

When the food was ready she attacked it with gusto. Everything tasted even better than it should have, as if her senses of taste and smell were more acute than normal, and she savored every bite.

When they could eat no more, they pushed their plates aside and went to sit on the edge of the pool, dangling their feet in the heated water as darkness fell and the stars popped out one by one.

"It's been a perfect day," she said dreamily as she idly kicked up water droplets with her toes.

"I'm glad you've enjoyed it. But I might be about to ruin it."

"Oh?" She eyed him curiously. The only way he would ruin it would be to send her home.

He looked everywhere but at her. "You see, the last time I found myself in this position was back in the dark ages, when men were expected to seduce and women were expected to guard their virtue."

"Or they pretended to," Keely added coyly. Her heart beat faster. She was grateful for the darkness that hid her blush.

"Right. So now that we've all reached this enlightened age, what's the politically correct way for a man to let a woman know that he wants her?"

"I, um, think you just did." She reached up to caress his angular jaw, urging him to join her in the kiss she craved. He wasted no time accepting her invitation, swiftly taking possession of her mouth with a thoroughness that left no doubt as to his intentions.

He had kissed her often during the past few weeks, and she had always responded with a burst of pent-up ardor followed by a cautionary drawing back. This time she met the heated seduction of his mouth with her usual eagerness and more, opening her mind to the taste and texture of him, the scent of his warm skin. And when he would have paused, allowing her breathing space, thinking space, she simply tilted her head and slanted her mouth against his at a different angle.

He made a small noise of approval deep in the back of his throat, holding her more tightly. She rubbed his nape, noticing with exquisite sensitivity how the short, silky hairs there tickled her palm.

"Tell me," she murmured against his lips, "what's the politically correct way for a woman to let a man know that she wants him as much as he wants her?"

"You just did." They shared one more kiss, softer, gentler, but no less evocative. "Let's go inside, or I might just make love to you right here on the concrete."

"You know what?" she asked as he pulled her to her feet. "I probably wouldn't have minded."

They made their way inside with a step-kiss-step cadence, leaving wet footprints behind them. Ben paused to turn out the lights in the family room. For a moment Keely was left standing alone in darkness, but then he was back, his strong arms around her, calming any fears that might have crept up on her.

She was glad when he made no move for the bedroom. Instead he led her to the big, inviting couch she'd seen but never sat on because they always seemed to find themselves in the kitchen. The couch had wonderfully puffy cushions, she soon discovered, and she sank into them as if she were an angel on a cloud, pulling him down with her.

That was as close as she got to being an angel.

Apparently in no hurry, he continued to kiss her as his hands made a leisurely exploration of her hills and valleys. Her body tightened in anticipation each time he skirted close to her aching breasts. Heat coiled through her, like a hot metal spring being stretched to its limit.

She couldn't remember ever wanting a man this way. Maybe she never had.

She made several attempts to get rid of their clothes, eager to feel skin against skin, hard and warm against soft and warmer, but he kept distracting her with devilish kisses to her ear, her neck, her collarbone. Finally she gave up and allowed him to run the show at his own pace. If she turned into a pile of ashes before they were done, so be it.

She'd never been with a man who wasn't eager to get on with the main event. Ben's lovemaking was new and exciting, like a fresh breeze in a stale room. There wasn't anything predictable about it, no orchestrated script to follow. He was as apt to kiss her on the nose or the knee as anywhere else. He went from a heavy-breathing intensity to light teasing and back again in the blink of an eye.

When he finally began to undress her, he still didn't rush. Instead he removed a piece of clothing from time to time, hers or his, in no particular order. If he found a place he wanted to kiss and something was in the way, off it came.

She found herself alternately laughing with unmitigated delight, then moaning with a different sort of pleasure when he swirled his tongue against the sensitive undersides of her breasts or caressed her inner thigh *just so*.

As he was in the process of covering her quivering midriff with a wide range of kisses, he paused and gazed at her. She could barely make out his soulful expression in the faint moonlight leaking through the miniblinds.

"What is it?" she asked.

"I should have asked you this earlier, but...you *are* protected, aren't you?"

She supposed she couldn't blame him for assuming that a woman committed to childlessness would naturally take precautions. At least he'd thought about it, and better late than never.

"Keely? If you're not I can—"

"It's taken care of," she cut in briskly. *And how.*

"Good." A definite note of relief tinged his voice. He resumed his sensual assault with renewed vigor, only to pause again after a few seconds. "What made you decide not to have children?"

Oh, Ben, not now, she wanted to say. Of all the rotten times to bring up this subject... She propped her head on her arm so she could see him better. "It's just a personal preference," she said, hoping he would take the bland reply as a hint.

He didn't. "But you're so good with kids."

"I love children," she replied evenly, trying to hold on to her patience. She felt like blurting out the truth. That would fix his wagon. It would also put an abrupt halt to their lovemaking.

She would have to tell him. There was no way around it. But surely she could find a better time than this.

She grasped his muscular shoulders and pulled herself up until she was nose to nose with him. "Would you forget about kids? In case you haven't noticed, you have a desperate woman on your couch who's on the verge of begging you to make love to her."

That made him smile wickedly. "Is that so? Guess I'll have to do something about that."

Keely sagged with relief as he resumed kissing her, and before long she again lost herself to Ben's touch. He drove every rational thought from her mind, leaving room only for sensations—the feel of his questing hands working their way lovingly over her body, the warmth of his breath fanning her hair, the low, soft sound of his voice when he murmured sweet words she couldn't quite understand.

Her panties were the last barrier between them. She gave a shaky sigh as he slid them down her legs and the cool air reached the hot, damp place between her legs.

Moonlight slanted in through the miniblinds, casting pale stripes over her body, and Ben paused to study the effect. His frank admiration made her squirm at first, especially when he began tracing the stripes with his finger across her abdomen, her ribs and her breasts.

"Don't be embarrassed," he said. "I have to look at you. I may never catch you in this light again."

"I'm not embarrassed," she assured him. "I'm just not used to anyone staring at me without my clothes on."

"Get used to it."

She liked the sound of that. "I think I can," she said through a smile. But the lightness vanished as desire renewed itself. God, how she wanted to be joined with him and give him everything she felt inside.

In perfect tune with her thoughts, he gently covered her body with his, insinuating his leg between hers. When he kissed her this time, it was an invitation and a plea.

"Yes," she said softly, opening herself to him.

She felt his hard flesh against her softness, questing, seeking entrance. She tilted her hips to a more accommodating angle. Even so, she tensed and gasped as he started to enter her.

Immediately he stopped. "What's wrong?"

"Nothing. Well, not much, anyway." Her voice wavered with uncertainty. "It's been so long, I guess I'm a little afraid."

"Afraid I'll hurt you?" He smoothed his hand over her hair with such infinite tenderness, the question seemed ludicrous.

"No. Just... afraid. Like I'm a virgin all over again. Pretty ridiculous, huh?"

"Not at all."

"Please, don't stop."

"Don't worry, I won't." But he withdrew and raised himself to his knees.

She almost whimpered in protest. "Then what are you—"

"I'm just switching gears." He threw aside a couple of pillows, then rearranged things so that he was lying on his back.

She felt like a slow child discovering the answer to an easy math problem when she finally realized his intention. At his silent urging she straddled his hips. When his arousal again came in contact with her softness, excitement shot through her. She was still apprehensive, but so hungry for fulfillment that she doubted anything could stop her from loving Ben.

"Now you have complete control," he said, rubbing her thighs from knee to hips with slow, sensual circles. Perhaps he intended to relax her, but the opposite was happening. "You can take things as slowly—or as fast—as you like."

She fully intended to do both. With his big hands around her hips, guiding but not pushing, she lowered herself with excruciating slowness, savoring the ever-growing sense of fullness. Whatever silly qualms she'd had dissipated as she took all of him into her. He rewarded her with a low groan that spoke of need.

Instincts as old as humankind prodded her to begin their dance of love. She rose up on her knees, unsheathing him, then settled against him, welcoming him home again. Soon the dance accelerated, from a sensual waltz to a fevered flamenco. She could almost hear the music that drove her.

With his eyes closed, savoring his own pleasure, Ben nonetheless continued to massage her, using his thumbs to create an exquisite pressure from her waist, down her belly to the soft nest of curls between her legs and back up again. His caress wandered dangerously close to the place that throbbed and tingled, making her want with a strength that was new to her. Then he did touch that vortex of her desires—lightly at first, fleetingly, then more firmly.

She surprised herself by crying out, but she had lost control. Driven solely by instinct, she rode him faster and harder until she drove herself right through an invisible wall and into a world of bright colors and dizzying heights and waves of pleasure so intense she thought she would die from them.

When the storm winds calmed she opened her eyes and saw the happiest, most satisfied expression she'd ever seen on a man's face. But it wasn't his own satisfaction that made him smile. He was purely enjoying her climax. Seconds later he gripped her fiercely and let go of his own control, and she realized with a pang of emotion that he had purposely held back so that he could watch her, and then she him.

It was over in seconds, but what seconds! She slumped forward, breathing hard, utterly spent. He wrapped his arms around her and breathed with her. They came back down to earth together.

Ben said nothing for a long time. He couldn't blame Keely for her earlier fears. If he had known making love with her would shake him to his core, he might have felt a bit apprehensive himself.

And to think, he'd almost blown it. What had come over him? Here was this beautiful woman, warm and eager in his arms. For weeks he had thought about this moment, wondering how she would feel, how she would respond. And then the moment had finally arrived, and just when they were both crazy with wanting he had started grilling her about her decision not to become a parent.

It was ridiculous. Why had her reasons suddenly held such keen interest for him? Although he definitely did not want more children, he found himself questioning the fact that this woman, who seemed to want to share so much with him, had ruled out the possibility of forging that special bond of parenthood with him.

So it was okay for him not to want children, but not okay for her? This was blatantly unfair to Keely. He must be crazy!

Oh, to hell with it. Whatever doubts he'd had, making love with her had driven them from his mind. This was right. This was the beginning of something rare. At that moment he promised himself he would never question her on the subject of children again.

He started to tell her how good it had been, then decided that wasn't necessary. She knew.

"Will you stay the night with me, Keely?" he asked instead.

"Yes." The single word packed a punch.

Feeling romantic, he carried her upstairs to the bedroom. He thought about making love to her again—Lord knows he could have. But the afterglow was so warm, so strong, he decided not to tamper with heaven.

Anyway, Keely was sleepy. Her eyelids drooped even as he snuggled her up against his shoulder and pulled a sheet over them.

The next thing Ben knew, the phone was ringing. Startled, disoriented, he squinted at the illuminated clock by the bed as he fumbled for the speaker phone. It was 2:30 a.m., he noted with irritation as he at last found the right button to push.

"Hello," he said gruffly.

"Daddy?"

He sat up, immediately alert to the note of despair in his daughter's voice. "Tina, what's wrong?"

Six

Keely awakened to the sound of Tina's tearful voice pouring from the speaker phone.

"Daddy, will you come get me, please?"

Ben grabbed the receiver. "Where are you?" he barked.

Keely couldn't hear Tina's response after that, but whatever the girl was saying, it made Ben fume. She could feel the heat of anger radiating from him.

"I'll be there as soon as I can," he said. "Don't move from that spot!" He slammed down the receiver.

"What happened?" Keely asked.

"She lied to me, that's what happened," Ben said with obvious disgust as he tossed the covers aside and sprang from the bed. He strode to the dresser and began pulling open various drawers in search of underwear, jeans, socks. "That's what I get for trusting her, another kick in the teeth."

With the bedspread wrapped around her, Keely shad-
owed his movements around the room. "Will you please
tell me what happened?"

"There was no 'lake weekend' with her friends. There
was just her and Todd and a key to the Paleys's empty lake
house. Now she's had a fight with Todd, that rotten little
hood, and she comes running back to Daddy. Well, she's
not getting any sympathy from me. If he dumped her and
left her stranded at some Smithville convenience store in
the middle of the night, it's no more than she deserves for
lying to me in the first place."

Alarm bells went off in Keely's head. If Tina was upset
enough to call her father and own up to the lie, something
really bad must have happened. And Keely had a pretty
good idea what it was.

"Ben, will you please calm down?"

"I don't want to calm down," he said as he headed out
the bedroom door with Keely trailing behind him. "She's
not going to get to me this time with her tears and her
apologies and her promises to be good. That girl is in big
trouble."

He ranted all the way down the stairs and into the family room, where he'd left his shoes. He sat down to put
them on. Keely quickly climbed into her own clothes,
which were strewn willy-nilly all over the room. She might
have been self-conscious, getting dressed in front of Ben
with the lights blazing and the room in disarray all around
them, a reminder of the passion they had unleashed here
just hours ago. But Ben wasn't paying any attention to the
room or to her.

"Ben, will you please listen to me?" she asked, pulling
her striped top over her head. "You have every right to be
angry, but you have to calm down and deal with this ra-
tionally. Yes, Tina lied, but she made the right decision by

calling you when things got too much for her to handle. If you lose your temper, you'll discourage her from ever coming to you with a problem again."

"Maybe I'll discourage her from lying, too."

"But she already knows she made a mistake," Keely argued as she slid her feet into her sandals. "Right now she's just a scared little girl reaching out to her father for comfort."

"'Scared little girl,' my foot!" Ben exploded. "It's an act, pure and simple, designed to get my sympathy and avoid punishment. And it's not going to work."

Keely wasn't so sure it was an act. If Tina were really intent on avoiding punishment, she wouldn't have called her father in the first place. But Ben wasn't in the mood to listen to reason. Keely could only hope that he would calm down during the drive to Smithville.

She grabbed her purse and followed Ben to the front door. He reached for the knob, then paused and turned toward her. Finally she saw the light of reason in his eyes.

"Keely, I'm sorry. This isn't your fault, and I didn't mean to yell at you."

"I didn't take it personally," she assured him.

"And I sure didn't want the evening to end this way. I wanted to fix us waffles for breakfast and read the comics together..."

"I'll take a rain check," she said with a fleeting smile. "Listen, why don't I go with you to pick up Tina?"

"Are you sure you want to? It won't be a pretty sight."

"Yes, I'm sure. Maybe I can help." She didn't add that she suspected Tina might need another woman's comfort.

"All right, but don't blame me if you get injured in the crossfire. You've never seen a full-blown Kinkaid family quarrel."

The tense twenty-minute drive to Smithville Lake did nothing to calm Ben down. It was as if he was determined to maintain a healthy head of steam, and he soundly rebuffed Keely's advice to deal with Tina reasonably.

They located the convenience store without much trouble, despite Tina's convoluted directions. When they pulled into the parking lot, they found her sitting on the curb with her arms resting across her knees and her head bent in a classic pose of dejection.

She glanced up and recognized her father's car. A brief look of relief crossed her face as she bounced to her feet, but she quickly schooled her features into a neutral expression.

To Ben's credit, he did ask the right question when he got out of the car. "Tina, are you okay?"

She nodded unconvincingly, then abruptly threw her arms around Ben's neck. "I'm sorry, Daddy," she sobbed. "I'm sorry, I'm sorry, I'm sorry."

Ben gave her a perfunctory hug in return, but his face was as hard and implacable as a piece of granite. "Get your things and get in the car."

Oh, Ben, Keely thought. He'd picked a helluva time to become a strict disciplinarian. Here was a chance to mend fences with his daughter, and he was going to blow it.

Tina picked up her canvas tote bag and started for the passenger door. She skidded to an abrupt halt when she saw Keely. "What's *she* doing here?" she demanded, making Keely wince.

"Just get in the car," Ben repeated, more wearily this time.

Tina reversed directions and climbed through Ben's door into the cramped back seat.

A tense silence reigned until they were out on the highway again. Then Ben demanded through clenched teeth, "Well, I'm waiting."

Keely could almost see Tina's hackles rising. "Waiting for what?" the girl responded, her words needle sharp.

"An explanation."

"I already *told* you what happened." Tina's voice rose higher with each word."

"Then tell me again."

Tina sighed with exasperation. "A bunch of kids were at the Paleys's house earlier, and I thought the girls were all going to stay over, but then everyone went home except me and Todd."

"And where were Mr. and Mrs. Paley?"

"Out of town."

"You knew that yesterday morning."

"Yes. I lied, all right?"

"No, it's not all right. I trusted you, just like all the times before, and you betrayed that trust, just like all the times before. When am I going to learn? Are you ever going to stop lying, Tina?"

"You wouldn't have let me go if I'd told you the Paleys weren't home."

"No kidding," Ben replied with a huff.

"It wasn't just me. A lot of the other kids didn't tell their parents the truth, either."

"But a lot of other kids didn't spend the night in an empty house with their boyfriends."

"I didn't spend the night!" Tina objected with surprising passion. "That's why I called you. Could you just try and understand instead of attacking?"

"All I understand is that my sixteen-year-old daughter is behaving like a—"

"Ben!" Keely broke in, unable to keep silent. "Please don't say something in the heat of anger that you'll regret."

"No, let him finish," Tina said. "I'm behaving like a what? Or is it a who? Like my mother, maybe?"

Keely tried again. "Tina, this is no time to let your sharp tongue get away from you. You're not improving the situation."

"Look, you stay out of this!" Tina lashed out. "Haven't you caused enough trouble?"

"I simply want the two of you to calm down and discuss this reasonably."

"How can you expect me to be reasonable," Ben argued, "when my daughter is a pathological liar? How can you even defend her? She looked you in the eye and told you she wasn't promiscuous."

She hadn't been, not at that point, Keely wanted to say. Of that she was fairly certain. But before she could formulate what she wanted to say, Tina took control of the argument.

"You're one to talk about promiscuous," she cried, jabbing her father in the shoulder. "Before you go making accusations, I suggest you look at who's sitting next to you in the front seat. I suppose you two were playing Monopoly when I called at two o'clock in the morning?"

Horrified, Keely hunched down in her seat and said nothing. What *could* she say?

Predictably, Ben had a retort. "What Keely and I do is none of your business."

"And what I do is none of yours."

"Oh, yes, it is. I'm the parent. You're the child. And as long as you're living under my roof I have every right to know what you're doing every second of every day. From now on, I intend to. You're grounded for the rest of your life. And I want you to quit that job at the video store."

"Fine! I'll join a convent!"

Keely couldn't keep quiet. "Ben, I think you're over-reacting."

"Stay out of this, Keely. I can handle it."

"With all the sensitivity of a bulldozer," she murmured, but he didn't hear her over the roar of the Porsche's powerful engine.

She folded her arms and said nothing on the remainder of the trip back to the Kinkaids' house. This had been a mistake all the way around. She should have gotten in her car and gone home, instead of driving to Smithville with Ben. She should have known that she was too closely involved with both of these people to be any help as a mediator.

When they arrived back at the house, Keely followed Ben and Tina inside, though she wasn't sure why. There wasn't much left to say or do.

Tina stormed to her basement bedroom and slammed the door behind her, leaving Keely alone with Ben.

"Well, that was a fun outing," she said.

"I warned you."

"Yes, you did," she agreed.

He came closer, close enough to touch, yet he didn't touch her. "I'm sorry the evening turned out like this, honey. And I'm sorry I snapped at you in the car. Tina just makes me so angry sometimes I forget what I'm doing."

"I can see that."

"Would you like me to take you home? I hate to think of you driving alone at this hour."

"I'll be fine."

"I'll call you tomorrow, then."

"No, I don't think you should."

Ben grew very still. "What?"

"You and Tina need some time to work things out. You'll never do that as long as I'm around. I've been a source of contention between you from the beginning. I couldn't live with myself if I created a permanent breach between you."

Ben appeared utterly bewildered. "How long . . . ?"

"I don't know. As long as it takes, I guess."

"I don't believe this. You can't bail out on me now, Keely, not when my daughter is in a state of mutiny."

"She wouldn't *be* in that state if you'd listened to me. You don't really want my help. You just want someone to blame in case you don't make the right decisions."

"Keely, how can you say that?"

She was ashamed of herself. She'd struck out unfairly at Ben solely because he had done the same. "I'm sorry. I know that's not true. Just the same, I've butted in for the last time. You and Tina will work things out much more easily on your own."

Ben pressed his mouth into a tight line. "Fine, if that's the way you feel. Good night, then." He turned and stomped up the stairs, in no less of a snit than Tina.

"Jeez," Keely said under her breath as she started for the door. But a faint sound halted her—the sound of crying.

She should ignore it and go. But she couldn't. With a sigh she went to the basement door and opened it a crack. "Tina? Are you really okay?"

"Go away," Tina sobbed.

Keely didn't listen. Instead she slipped through the door and made her way down the stairs into the shadowy room. A single, dim bulb in a bedside lamp revealed Tina sprawled on her stomach across the huge bed, clutching a stuffed dog. Her shoulders shook and she tried to cry quietly. Keely sat on the edge of the bed and wordlessly rubbed Tina's back in a soothing circular motion.

"I don't need therapy," Tina said in a muffled voice.

"No, but you could probably use a friend. I'm not your counselor anymore, Tina. I'm just a woman. But I've been through this before, and you might be surprised at how well I understand."

"Understand what?"

Keely hesitated. What if she was wrong? She decided to ask point blank. "This *was* your first time tonight, wasn't it?"

Tina looked up at her and blinked, the tears subsiding for the moment. "How did you know that?"

"Because you look exactly how I felt when it happened to me."

Tina thought about this for a moment. "Dad doesn't know. He thinks I've been sleeping with Todd for a long time."

"Men are idiots. Sometimes," Keely added as an afterthought. She didn't feel like a responsible adult right now, and it was hard to censor herself.

"You can say that again," Tina agreed.

"So was it awful?"

"It was the pits! I thought he loved me, but all he wanted was to get in my pants. He was rough, and it hurt, and when it was over he acted like it was no big deal." She started crying again.

Keely pulled the girl against her shoulder and held her, rocking her gently until she was cried out. Poor, motherless baby. Who else could she turn to? Certainly not her father. Even if Ben had been inclined to listen sympathetically, there were some things a man simply couldn't understand.

"Oh, honey, it won't always be that bad, I promise," she said, thinking she'd like to get hold of that Todd and slap him silly. First times didn't have to be awful. He could have been gentle and patient—the way Ben had been when faced with Keely's own virginlike qualms.

"It would have to get better," Tina said, laughing through the last of her tears. "If it was always like this, people wouldn't do it so much." At last she pulled away from Keely and found a box of tissues. She mopped her face and blew her nose. "You aren't gonna make me tell Dad, are you?" she asked abruptly.

Keely had to think about this one. It was second nature for her to advise that Tina tell the truth. But if she were in the girl's shoes, she would lie through her teeth. "You do whatever you feel most comfortable with," she finally said. "Um, Tina, you did use protection, didn't you?"

Much to Keely's relief, the girl nodded. Then a look of puzzlement came over her face. "How come you're being so nice to me, when I haven't been very nice to you?"

"Because I like you," Keely answered without hesitation. "I guess I keep hoping someday you'll like me back."

"I don't *not* like you," Tina said, studying her fingernails. "I'll even try to be nicer about you and Dad going out."

"That's something you won't have to worry about. Your father and I aren't going to be seeing each other anymore, at least, not for a while."

Tina looked up with round, startled eyes. "Why not?"

Keely hedged. "Several reasons. Listen, I need to get going," she said quickly, before she was the one crying. "Are you all right now?"

Tina nodded. "Yeah. Thanks."

"No problem," Keely replied with a smile. "If you want to talk, give me a call at home. I'm in the book. If not me, then talk to someone. Promise?"

"I will."

As she left, Keely wished there was someone *she* could talk to, someone who could ease her own breaking heart.

Summer was traditionally the time of year Keely "recharged her batteries," and this summer was no exception. She counseled very few students, so most of her time was her own. She spent hours every day in her small backyard, planting and weeding and clipping until it looked good enough to be showcased in some slick magazine.

On this late July morning she was rearranging the rocks around a stone birdbath to make more room for some rapidly growing mock-orange bushes she'd planted earlier in the spring. It was hot, hard work, and she found herself pausing and resting more often than was usual.

"Need some help?"

She looked up with a start to see a tall, wonderfully familiar figure standing on her deck in khaki shorts and a purple knit shirt. Tanned and strong looking, with the sun glinting gold off his hair, he made a heart-stopping picture.

"Ben!" she cried, unable to hide the pleasure in her voice. She hurried across the yard to join him, heedless of her less-than-flattering garden smock or the sweat that dampened her hair. Although they had talked on the phone a couple of times, two months had passed since she'd actually seen him.

Midway across the yard she almost stumbled, and she stopped to get her bearings. Could the mere sight of a gorgeous man actually make a woman dizzy?

"Keely! Are you okay?" Ben hurried down the deck stairs just as she looked up with a reassuring smile.

"I'm fine," she said. "It's just this heat. I've been working too hard, I think, and I skipped breakfast."

He slipped an arm around her shoulders. "Let's go inside where it's cool and get you something to drink," he said. "That is, if I'm welcome inside," he added. "I wasn't sure you'd want to see me."

"Of course I do." Unable to stop herself, she put her arms around him and hugged him hard. God, how she'd missed him. The strength of his body against hers sent a familiar tingle coursing through her, a faint echo of the desire he was capable of bringing to life. As always, he smelled wonderful, like citrus and soap. "Sorry," she said, pulling away. "I'm getting you all grimy."

He laughed softly. "Don't apologize. I'll take a little grime for a hug like that, any day. Come on." He urged her up the steps and through the sliding glass door.

They settled at the breakfast bar with tall glasses of lemonade. Keely emptied half of hers in one series of gulps.

"Are you feeling better?" Ben asked, worry creasing his forehead.

"I'm fine. It was just a moment of light-headedness. Now tell me, what are you doing here?"

"I'm working on a pool just a couple of miles from here, so I decided to take my lunch break and check up on you. I...I just couldn't stay away any longer, Keely. I miss you."

His words sent a healing warmth radiating through her body. "I miss you, too," she murmured. "How's Tina?"

Ben smiled. "She's great."

"The new job is turning out okay?" A few weeks ago, Ben had told her that he'd talked Tina into quitting the video store and working the summer for him. She would make more money and he could keep an eye on her.

"She loves it! Once she got over being mad at me, she found out she likes landscaping. She's healthy and tan and she smiles the whole time she's working. Of course, that might have something to do with the other kid who's on my summer crew. He's eighteen, blond-haired, blue-eyed—and he doesn't ride a motorcycle, thank God."

"I'll bet he wouldn't dare fool around with the boss's daughter, either," Keely added.

"You got that right. Seriously, Tina and I are getting along better than we have in months. Ever since that night she's been...well, not a model child, but a tolerable one."

"I'm glad," Keely said. "I did the right thing by staying away."

"Maybe." He frowned. "Was Tina the only reason you stopped seeing me?"

"What other reason could there be?"

"I thought maybe the, uh, intimacy frightened you just a little. Maybe you weren't ready. I didn't mean to rush you, Keely. In fact—"

"Oh, no," she interrupted. "You didn't rush me. I was ready. I wasn't frightened. Excited, nervous maybe, but never frightened. It was wonderful..." She cut herself off with a sip of lemonade before she embarrassed herself by gushing.

His smile was one of pure male satisfaction. "I thought so, too," he said softly. "Will you see me again?"

"I want to, Ben. But I'd hate to ruin things between you and Tina when you're just getting back on even footing again. Maybe in another—"

"Tina is the one who sent me here. She said she was tired of me being grouchy, and that she knew exactly what it would take to improve my disposition. She was right."

Keely raised one skeptical eyebrow. "Are you telling me your daughter wouldn't mind if you and I..."

"We have her blessing. She even offered to call you if you needed convincing, but I told her I could handle the negotiations. How am I doing so far?"

Keely's heart beat furiously. "Not bad," she said cautiously. With a few words he had changed the tenor of her summer...maybe her whole life. She was afraid to believe it could happen this fast, this easily.

"Any suggestions for improvement?"

"Well, you could...kiss me."

In a moment he was off his bar stool and had pulled Keely off hers. He gave her no opportunity to renege on her offer. Wrapping his arms securely around her, he claimed her mouth with his. The full force of two months' pent-up desire exploded between them.

The passionate onslaught made Keely's head spin. At first she met it with a warm and lively response. But when the initial, giddy sensation evolved into downright dizziness, she had to pull away.

"Keely, what's wrong?" Ben asked, his voice filled with concern.

She looked at him, gasping for breath and trying to focus on those changeable, green-gold eyes. His face was no more than a blur. "Haven't you ever made a girl swoon before?" she asked as her knees buckled and blackness engulfed her.

When she came to she found herself in an undignified sprawl on the dining room carpet. Her face was wet and sticky. Ben leaned over her with an empty glass in one hand, patting her face with the other. His brow was creased with worry.

"Did you just pour lemonade on me?" she demanded with the haughtiness of a duchess.

"Oh, thank God. You fainted! It was the handiest thing. How do you feel?"

"Lousy," she said as she regained her senses. She'd never fainted in her life, and she didn't like the feeling of disorientation.

Ben helped her to sit up, then scooped her into his arms.

"What are you doing?"

"Taking you to the hospital."

"You will do no such thing. Put me down!"

"It's not normal to pass out, Keely. Someone needs to take a look at you."

She would have argued more stridently, except that she agreed. She'd been feeling peculiar for a couple of weeks now, alternately nauseated and light-headed. She'd attributed the symptoms to the unusual heat, though she'd never been sensitive to heat before.

"Put me down," she said again in a more reasonable voice this time. "There's no sense rushing to an emergency room. Let me call my doctor and see if she'll squeeze me in this afternoon." She figured her doctor, never an alarmist, would schedule an appointment for her later in the week.

Ben did as Keely asked, though he grumbled. He stuck to her side like flypaper as she made the phone call, alert in case she should get another case of the head spins.

Pat McCommas, her doctor and a long-time friend, insisted that Keely come to the office immediately. Reluctantly Keely agreed, although she did take the time to mop the sticky lemonade off her face and to change from her muddy gardening smock.

"You don't have to come with me," she argued as Ben escorted her out the door, a proprietary hand at her waist. "I feel fine now. Pat's office is five minutes away."

"Save your breath. You are *not* getting behind the wheel of a car until your doctor says you can." With that he handed her into the passenger seat of his car.

She should have been irritated by his high-handedness, but frankly, she didn't mind him taking control. She was scared now, especially after hearing the anxious note in Pat's voice.

The afternoon dragged on interminably. First there was a forty-five minute delay in the waiting room. Then there was the cold examining room, where a nurse poked and prodded and asked endless questions. Finally there was Dr. McCommas herself, who, though not much older than Keely, seemed wise beyond her years. Keely felt better the moment Pat smiled at her.

There was more poking, more prodding, more questions, though Keely didn't mind them so much from Pat. Then the doctor told her she could get dressed and slipped from the room.

A cold knot of apprehension sat heavy in Keely's stomach as she pulled on her clothes. Why hadn't Pat said anything? She hadn't voiced any suspicions, nor had she made any assurances. That wasn't like her.

As Keely stepped into her sandals her doctor returned, wearing an unreadable expression. When she spoke, her voice was shaky. "Keely, I don't quite know how to tell you this . . ." she began.

Keely's heart rose into her throat. "Just tell me. I have some horrible disease, right?"

"Not unless you consider a baby a horrible disease."

Seven

Keely's head spun and her legs wobbled. She had no choice but to plunk down in the room's only chair. "You mean I'm p-pregnant?" she squeaked. "No way. That can't be. Pat, you *know* that's impossible. What about the scar tissue and the blocked tubes and all that other stuff?" she asked desperately.

Pat shrugged helplessly. "An hour ago, I would have voiced the same doubts. But apparently one of your eggs was determined enough to get through the scar tissue blockage and do its thing. I told you years ago that it *could* happen—"

"And that the odds against it were a million to one," Keely finished for her. Involuntarily her hand went to her flat abdomen. "Are you sure there's no mistake? I mean, I don't want to get all excited about this and then find out—"

"There's no mistake."

Keely was silent for a long time, staring down at her lap as the news soaked in. When she looked up at her doctor, she was grinning through a film of tears. "I feel like part of a miracle."

"Then you're happy about it?"

"Oh, yes," Keely answered without hesitation. "You know how badly I've wanted a baby."

"Ten years ago I knew it. Circumstances have changed since then."

"Not that. I still want to be a mother more than anything."

"And the father? How will he feel about this?"

"The father?"

"I'm assuming you didn't accomplish this miracle alone."

"Oh." Keely came to earth with a thud. "Oh, my God, Ben. He's sitting out in the waiting room." Feeling panicky, she jumped out of her chair and grabbed Pat's arm. "What am I going to tell him?"

A worried frown creased Pat's forehead. "You don't think he'll be pleased?"

"Pleased? He'll freak. He doesn't want more children. I told him I was protected."

"Then he'll have to adjust, won't he?" The doctor put a comforting arm around Keely's shoulders. "Don't let him spoil it for you. If he's any kind of good guy at all, he'll learn to like the idea."

Keely didn't know whether to laugh or cry.

Ben struggled to concentrate on the dog-eared magazine in his lap, but celebrity gossip paled in interest when compared to Keely's welfare. What the hell was taking so long?

The door to the inner office opened for about the twentieth time since Ben had sat down. Each time it did, he looked up anxiously. This time he was rewarded by the sight of Keely coming through to the waiting room. The look on her face was hard to interpret—relief? Panic? A number of emotions flickered in her eyes as their gazes caught and held.

He came out of his chair and crossed quickly to her. "Are you okay?" he asked worriedly, heedless of the stares from the other patients in the waiting room.

"I'm fine," she said in a monotone as she pulled out her checkbook to pay the receptionist.

He waited an eternity for her to finish the transaction, realizing that Keely would want some privacy before she revealed her diagnosis. Or she might not want to talk about it, even to him. Just because he witnessed her fainting spell and dragged her here didn't give him the right to know the details of her health.

Nonetheless, once they were outside the doctor's office, he tried again. "So what happened? Dr. McCommas couldn't find anything wrong?"

"Nothing's wrong, exactly." She paused in the middle of the hallway and laid a hand on his arm. "Ben, I'll tell you everything, and it'll probably be way more than you ever wanted to hear, but I have to do it in my own way, in my own time. Okay?"

"Okay, but...you're all right, aren't you?" The thought that she might be seriously ill made his stomach churn.

She flashed him a beatific smile. "I'm perfectly healthy. It's you I'm worried about."

"Huh?"

"Could we go get some lunch? I'm starving. Oh, but you probably need to get back to work."

"The crew can get along without me. This is more important."

Keely said nothing more until they were seated in a quiet back booth at a popular bar-and-grill not far from her house. Even then, she still waited until the waitress had come and gone and every conceivable subject of small talk was exhausted before launching into her explanation.

"Do you remember what I told you about why my marriage broke up?" she finally asked.

Ben scratched his chin, wondering what the hell this had to do with anything. "Yeah. He wanted children and you didn't."

"Well, there was a little more to it than that. The fact was, I *couldn't* have children. My tubes were hopelessly blocked with scar tissue. Jeff knew that when we got married and he seemed to accept it. But a few years later he changed his mind."

"And he divorced you because of that?" Ben was horrified. To divorce a woman because she didn't *want* children was one thing, but to abandon her because she was sterile was inexcusable. He felt an illogical urge to track down that weasely ex-husband of hers and break his face.

"It was a mutual decision. He was unhappy, and I knew he would find more satisfaction with a woman who could give him children, so... anyway, that part doesn't matter now."

The waitress picked that moment to bring their meal. Ben did no more than sample the cheese soup and pick at his Philly sandwich. He was too absorbed in what Keely had just told him to appreciate the food.

All along, he'd thought it odd that Keely claimed not to want children. She seemed like such a natural-born nurturer. Now he understood why she'd left his house in such a hurry that first time she came over. He had made some insensitive wisecrack about the fact that she didn't have children of her own. Her reticence to become involved with him made more sense, now, too. Some stupid man had labeled her "incomplete" or "inadequate," and she'd bought into the lie.

"Why didn't you tell me this before?" he asked gently. "It would have made a lot more sense than all that garbage about you not *wanting* children."

"I wanted to tell you, and I fully intended to." Her eyes pleaded for understanding. "But it's not something you blurt out. It's an extremely sensitive subject with me. More than once, a man has walked out of my life when he found out the truth. I needed to know you well and trust you first."

"Trust me?"

"Trust you enough to know that it wouldn't change the way you look at me."

"Oh, Keely." He reached across the table and took her hand. He wanted to take away all the hurt inflicted by all those bastards who had made her feel she was less than whole. "Of course it doesn't change the way I look at you, or feel about you. I've told you several times, I don't want more—"

She jerked her hand out of his grasp. "Don't say that!"

"Don't say what? I mean, even if I did want—"

"Shh!"

"But I would never—"

"Shut *up,* Ben."

"Okay." He shrugged and returned his attention to his cooling soup. Women were strange. Here he thought Keely was the most sane, practical, down-to-earth female he'd ever met, and she was behaving about as logically as Tina. What could be wrong with his reiterating that he doesn't want children?

Unless . . . *Oh, no.*

He looked up and found her staring at him, her big eyes filled with apprehension. Their gazes locked for several heartbeats. "I see you've figured it out," she said.

"You mean to tell me you're having a . . ." He couldn't quite bring himself to say the word.

"Baby," she finished for him, just before polishing off the last bit of her club sandwich.

"H-h-how?"

"The usual way. I didn't use any kind of birth control when we . . . because I didn't think there was any need. Dr. McCommas is beside herself. She said that by conceiving I overcame astronomical odds."

He didn't know what to say. He felt as if he'd been kicked in the gut, unable to breathe, unable to react except to gape in total shock. Then a sort of comforting numbness fell over him until the whole thing seemed unreal—as if he were watching a movie.

One glance told him how Keely felt. She was glowing, smiling a secret smile of satisfaction that had nothing to do with the meal she'd just inhaled.

He tried to imagine what she would look like with a huge stomach, huge with *his* child. The thought gave him a fleeting sense of warmth, quickly overtaken by cold, hard fear.

He wasn't ready to be a new father! Kids were hell on parents. He only had to think of Tina and the miles she'd put on him.

"Ben? I didn't expect you to do handsprings, but . . ."

"I'm sorry, Keely, I'm at a loss. I never imagined myself in this situation. Could you give me a few minutes to get used to the idea?"

She smiled weakly. "I suppose that's the least I could do. If it's any consolation, I didn't take the news gracefully myself. Pat almost had to scrape me off the floor."

"You seem to have recovered all right." He was almost jealous of her calm acceptance.

"Then I'm a good actress. I'm definitely still a little shell-shocked. But I might as well just tell you…I'm happy about it, and I'm anxious to know how you feel."

Ben took a deep breath. "Look, I let you break the news in your own sweet time. Let me react in mine, okay?"

"Okay," she said, blushing furiously. "I guess I'm not very good at this. I've never done it before."

Ben laid some money on the table. He was making a wretched mess of this whole thing. He wanted to pull Keely into his arms, tell her he was ecstatic about the baby and that everything would be fine. She didn't deserve his ambivalence, not when this should have been one of the happiest moments of her life. But he couldn't bring himself to fake an emotion he didn't feel. Dammit, he was confused.

Nothing more was said until they were seated in Ben's car. It was like an oven inside. Ben opened the windows and turned on the air conditioning full blast. Then he calmly said, "You want to get married, I assume. When do you want to do it?"

Keely looked at him blankly.

"Surely you don't think I would expect you to raise the child by yourself?"

"I consider it an honor and a privilege to raise this child, not some odious obligation," she said in a hurt voice. "Ben, regardless of how you feel, I want this baby, marriage or not. Maybe that's selfish of me, I don't know, but it's like I've been given a second chance, a whole new life, almost. And if you don't want any part of it, well, that's just fine. I would never force you to—"

"Whoa! Did I say you were forcing me? Do you actually think, if given the choice, that I would just walk away from a child of my blood? I'm not a barbarian. I just told you I'd marry you."

She gave him a look that was downright bitter. "Yes, and what a lovely proposal it was. By the tone of your voice, you rank marrying me right up there with having a root canal."

"Keely, what do you want me to do?"

She sighed. "Right now, I want you to take me home. This heat is killing me."

"At least I can do that right," he muttered.

By the time they'd reached Keely's house, Ben was regretting every word he'd uttered over the past hour. He'd tried to do the right thing, the responsible thing, and instead he had somehow hurt and disappointed Keely.

This whole thing was such a shock. He needed time—time to adjust, to decide how he felt and what he should do.

Keely was of a like mind. "Let's give it a day or two to sink in," she said as she opened the car door.

He walked her inside over her protests. "I'll call you tomorrow," he said, standing awkwardly in the open doorway.

"Whenever you're ready."

After a cool shower, Keely lay on her bed in front of a fan, letting the blowing air dry the remaining moisture from her body. It was too hot to put on clothes and she was too drained to make the effort.

What a day this had been. She felt as if she'd been torn in two. Part of her was bursting with joy over her pregnancy. Another part of her cringed in pain at the way Ben had received the news.

Of all the men in the world who could have fathered her child, she had to pick one who was dead set against fatherhood! She sighed. She didn't want some other man to share this bond with her. She wanted Ben. But she also wanted him to welcome and love the child as well as her.

She already loved it, after knowing of its existence for only a few hours, and it was still no bigger than a lima bean.

She expected too much, she decided practically. She'd been given a baby. Maybe asking for the perfect father with the perfect attitude was pushing her luck.

Reaching for the phone, she decided to share her news with someone who would accept it with unqualified joy. Her older sister, Eileen, knew the pain Keely had gone through when she had come to terms with her infertility. In fact, more than once Eileen had acted as if she felt guilty because she'd managed to have three healthy boys while Keely had no children.

Eileen's reaction was everything Keely had hoped. "A baby!" she squealed into the phone. "After all this time. How wonderful! You must be beside yourself. When's it due?"

"Late February."

"And are you healthy? Is everything okay? Do you have morning sickness?" The questions came in rapid-fire succession.

"Apparently I'm okay, although I did faint today. That's why I went to the doctor. When she told me I was pregnant, I almost fainted again. I never even suspected, although I have been queasy the past couple of mornings. My doctor gave me a diet to follow and some vitamins, and she wants to monitor the pregnancy closely because of my age."

"Your age? I had one at thirty-seven!"

"I know. It's just a precaution."

"So, how is Ben taking the news?" Eileen asked. "Ben, that's his name, right? The pool guy?" When Keely didn't answer right away, she said, "You have told him, haven't you?"

"I told him. He's shocked." That was about all Keely could give him.

"But he's going to marry you, right?"

"Well . . . he offered, but I didn't accept."

"*What?* Keely, are you nuts? You can't have a baby by yourself, not when there's a perfectly respectable father standing by with a ring."

"Lots of single women have babies," Keely countered, automatically defensive. "The only reason Ben offered to marry me—grudgingly, I might add—was that he feels obligated. He's been divorced for years, and he already has a daughter almost grown. He doesn't want to start over with a brand-new family."

"But it's as much his responsibility—"

"He did take responsibility," Keely interrupted. "Before we went to bed, he offered to take precautions but I assured him I was protected. Besides, I don't intend to cut him off from the child. I'm just not going to force marriage and parenthood down his throat. Lord knows it's hard enough to keep a marriage together when two people are in love and committed."

"But don't you love him?" Eileen asked in a small voice.

Yes. With all her heart. "The question is, does he love me? I don't think so." Keely forced herself to sound matter-of-fact. If Ben did love her, he would have told her so. He would gladly accept the child who was the product of their love.

"I guess I wouldn't want to marry without love," Eileen finally agreed. "And there's really no reason to force the issue because of a baby. You're right, single mothers are everywhere today. There's not much of a stigma attached to it anymore, at least, not in Kansas City."

"Oh, dear," Keely said as a frightening thought occurred to her. "Not in Kansas City, but what about in Desmond?" Desmond was the small town where her parents lived, where Keely and Eileen had grown up. It was less than twenty miles from Eileen's farm.

"You know Mother and Dad will be supportive," Eileen hedged.

"But I'll embarrass them. With Dad and his Rotary Club, and Mother with the Library Guild—they're so visible! They won't be able to hide a single daughter with a baby."

"You know they would never want to hide you, no matter what. If they're a little embarrassed, they'll survive. Anyway, don't think about that now. Don't let it ruin your happiness. You're going to be a mommy. Everything else will work out, somehow."

"You're right," Keely said, smiling again. It was hard not to smile, despite the hurdles she would face in the future. The unborn child had faced worse obstacles just getting itself conceived.

"Of course I'm right," Eileen quipped. "I'm the oldest. I always know better."

"Oh, please," Keely moaned. "Don't start with the—oops, there's the doorbell and I'm lying here stark naked."

"I'll let you go, then. Keep me posted."

Keely quickly hung up and slid off the bed, then groped through her closet for a robe, only mildly irritated over the interruption. Her sister had made her feel much better.

Just knowing that the baby would have one doting aunt meant a lot. No matter what, the kid wouldn't come into the world unwanted or unloved. Thank God for family, she thought as she hastily jerked the terry robe over her nakedness and hurried to the door.

When she opened it, she found Ben standing on her front porch, looking as penitent as a whipped dog. He also looked sexy as hell. He'd changed from work clothes to a pair of crisp, new-looking jeans and a pale blue cotton shirt that stretched invitingly over his wide shoulders.

"What are you doing here?" she blurted out. "I thought you were going to call me tomorrow."

"I don't need till tomorrow," he said. "I've had plenty of time to think about everything, and I know what I want. Um, you're letting all your air conditioning outside."

"Oh. I guess you'd like to come in." Feeling dazed, she let him in and shut the door. She wasn't sure she was ready for this. "What have you got behind your back?"

"Oh, this?" He handed her a slim crystal vase that held two red roses. "One for you and one for the baby," he murmured, staring down at his shoes.

Keely's eyes filled with tears as she accepted the flowers. This was the sweetest gift anyone had ever given her. She raised on her toes and kissed his cheek. "Thank you." She noticed that his face was satin smooth and scented with after-shave. He'd gone to some trouble for her.

"Let's sit in the living room. It's cooler in there," she suggested, though she now *knew* she wasn't ready for another emotional discussion. After this roller coaster of a day, she was about as sharp as oatmeal.

She sat down on the love seat, while he took the wing chair next to it. He was close enough to touch, but Keely refrained. Instead she pulled nervously at the hem of her short robe and waited for Ben to say what he'd come to say.

"I thought I needed time to get used to the idea of having another child," he began. "But as soon as I had a few moments to myself, everything became clear. All I had to do was think back to Nora's pregnancy."

Keely crossed her arms and waited for him to continue.

"I was a lot more naive about having children back then, so even though we hadn't planned to have a baby so soon, I was crazy about the idea. Nora, however, was less than enthusiastic. I remember exactly how that made me feel—angry, defensive, hurt. I didn't understand how she could possibly resent a child of our flesh. I must have made you feel exactly the same way."

Keely couldn't deny it, so she said nothing.

"Of course she went through with it," he continued. "Whether for me or for appearances' sake, I don't know, but she had Tina and she even pretended to be happy about it, for a while. But I knew different, and so did Tina.

"Nora and I stayed together for seven long years after that, supposedly for Tina's sake. But I know now, Tina would have been better off with no mother than with one who alternately ignored her or reminded her that she was an unwanted burden."

A cold lump of fear lodged in Keely's chest. "So what does this mean?" she couldn't help asking. "Are you saying our baby will be better off without a—"

"No! Oh, Keely, honey, I didn't mean that. My point is, Nora's attitude hurt me as much as it did Tina. It destroyed our marriage. And I don't want that to happen to us. The things I said this afternoon must have hurt you terribly, and I'm sorry. I was just so surprised and confused..."

"And you still are," Keely said quietly.

"No, I'm not. I know what I want. I want to marry you, Keely. It's what's best for everyone involved."

Keely closed her eyes and visualized the glittering prize he held out to her, right within her grasp. Marriage to Ben. At last, the happy family life she'd always dreamed of. But what if his dream turned into a nightmare? The situation with Nora he'd described did more to scare her than sway her to his way of thinking.

"I can't let you go through this pregnancy alone," he said when she made no comment. "You deserve a husband who will take care of you. And I won't allow a child of mine to be born out of wedlock. He or she deserves a father, a full-time father."

That's not good enough, she thought. *What about love?*

"Let me ask you something," she said. "And I want you to answer honestly. If not for the baby, would you want to marry me?"

He looked thoughtful for several moments, as if weighing how truthful he could afford to be. "Honestly? Uh..."

"That's what I thought," she said, her heart sinking.

"Wait a minute. All right, no, I hadn't specifically thought of asking you to marry me before today. But the past two months without you have been hell, Keely. And I had come to the conclusion that I wanted to have a serious, long-term relationship with you. That's a step in the right direction. Eventually I would have proposed. The 'little visitor' simply moved up the timetable a bit."

"'Little visitor,'" she repeated, smiling despite herself. She hadn't heard that old-fashioned term in years. She said nothing else for a few moments as she pondered the rest of his words.

Was he sincere about all this? Or was he just being honorable? Ben Kinkaid had a strong sense of responsibility. She knew that from his dealings with Tina. He might be merely saying whatever he thought it would take to get her to agree to marriage, because he really did believe it was the best thing for all involved.

Was she crazy to even consider turning him down? To submit her family to embarrassment because of some silly ideal she had about love and happiness? To bring her child into the world fatherless and doom it to a single-parent upbringing because *she* insisted on a fairy-tale romance?

Face it, Keely, she told herself sternly. She could do much worse than Ben Kinkaid as a husband and father to her baby. Maybe he didn't love her. Maybe he never would. He might not be a hundred percent committed to the idea of marriage and parenthood. But he would try to do what was right.

Surely a reluctant father was better than no father at all. And, who knows, perhaps he would warm up to the new family, once he got used to it.

"Okay," she said.

He gave her a blank look. "Okay, what?"

"Okay, Ben Kinkaid, I will marry you."

For a stunned moment, Ben just sat there, staring at her. Had he changed his mind already? Finally he flashed a tentative grin. "Good. Now, come here."

She gave a squeal of mild protest as he pulled her off the love seat and into his lap and gave her an exultant smack of a kiss—a victory kiss, she surmised. Her robe was askew, revealing all of one thigh and most of one breast. She squirmed in an effort to straighten out the garment.

"Oh, hold still and let me hug you," he scolded. "It's not every day a guy gets himself engaged. Anyway, your virtue's safe with me."

She grew still. "Is it?" she asked, unable to hide her disappointment.

"For now," he said, although he trailed one finger across her collarbone and down, skimming the top of her breast and making her shiver. "I figure you've had about all of me you can stand for one day."

She started to protest. A lifetime of Ben wouldn't be enough to satisfy her. But maybe he was right. This had been a helluva day. There would be plenty of time for them to ease back into the fragile physical intimacy they'd barely established two months ago.

"So, when do you want to do the deed?" Ben asked. "We could get the license tomorrow, but then I think we have to wait three days—"

"Wait a minute. I'm not going to skulk off to some justice of the peace. If we're going to do this thing, I want it done right. I eloped the first time, and I promised my family I would never do that again. I want a wedding with a minister and flowers and a cake."

"Okay, no problem," Ben said, laughing. "How long will it take to put together this extravaganza? Don't take too long, or we might end up with an extra little guest."

"I can do it in a month," she declared. "Don't worry, I'll keep it simple and tasteful, since it's a second wedding for both of us. But I have to have a bridesmaid or two. My sister would kill me if she didn't get to be matron of honor. What about your family?" she asked, getting into the spirit of the thing. "Who would you like to include in the wedding party?"

He thought for a moment. "Well, I don't have any brothers or sisters, but there is one thing I'd like. Could you find something special for Tina to do?"

Keely gasped. "Tina! Oh, my God, I forgot all about her. She's going to *hate* this!"

"No, she won't," Ben argued, though not very forcefully. "She'll simply have to get used to the idea."

"Ben, it's taken her months to accept the idea of you and me just *dating*. How is she going to feel when I move into your house with all my stuff? And then the baby...it's going to turn her life upside down. Oh, dear, I hadn't even considered her feelings in all this. I'm not sure . . ."

"Don't get cold feet, not yet. Hell, we haven't even been engaged ten minutes. You worry about the wedding. I'll take care of Tina."

Keely took Ben's hand and squeezed it. "No. We'll tell her together. And we'll deal with her reaction together. From now on, that's how it has to be. Agreed?"

He nodded grimly. "Agreed."

Eight

Ben and Keely enticed Tina to spend time with them the following Saturday by offering a breakfast treat she couldn't refuse—chocolate croissants. Together they planned to break the news of the impending marriage and the "blessed event" to follow. But Tina didn't make it easy on them. She smelled the trap.

"So, what's with all this sudden togetherness?" she asked, just before taking a huge bite out of a gooey pastry. She sat sprawled in a chair on the patio, where a rare, cool morning had beckoned them to enjoy their breakfast. "Seems to me, since you guys haven't seen each other for a couple of months, the last person you want hanging around is me."

She didn't say it in a sullen, spiteful way, Ben noted with some relief. She was just being her usual high-spirited, ornery self. Now that she'd gotten over being angry at Keely's intrusion into their lives, her attitude was one of amusement. The idea of her father in the throes of a sticky romance tickled her funny bone. The fact that school wasn't in session had taken some of the pressure off, too. Tina didn't have to worry about what her friends would think of her father dating a "teacher"—at least, not until fall.

"Well, Tina, as long as you brought it up," Ben began, but then he didn't quite know how to continue. He looked to Keely, silently pleading for support.

"Um, I'm sure you know that your father and I have grown very close over the past few months..." Keely said. "Even during the time we didn't see each other, we still felt, um..."

"Connected," Ben said.

"Yes, that's it," Keely agreed.

"It's very rare that two people feel that way," Ben continued, "and when they do—"

"Oh, puh-leeze!" Tina exploded, throwing up her hands in disgust. "I'm not seven years old. You don't have to give me a lecture on true romance. I get the picture. You two are in *love,*" she said in a singsong voice, accompanied by an energetic flutter of eyelashes. "And you want to get married. What are you asking me for? If you're looking for my blessing, you can forget it. I don't want or need a new mother, thank you very much." She bolted out of her chair and stalked away, leaving behind her half-eaten croissant.

"Tina, wait!" Ben barked, coming out of his chair. His command halted her as she reached for the sliding glass door, but she didn't turn around. "We're not done yet. We're not asking for your blessing, although that would be nice. We just feel you have a right to know what's going on, and why, since this is going to affect your life, too."

Tina's stance softened. Her tense shoulders relaxed and her hands, bunched unconsciously into fists, opened slightly.

"You don't have to be happy about this," Ben said in a lower voice, sensing victory. "You can be as angry and upset as you like. It's only natural that you would be upset when there's a major change coming into your life that you don't have any control over. I only demand one thing of you—that you listen to all the facts first. There are several important things we want you to know."

With a sigh she returned to the patio table. She swiveled her chair around and straddled it, then leaned her chin on her forearms in an attitude of studied indifference. "Okay, I'm listening."

Ben felt too nervous to sit. Now that they had Tina's undivided attention, he was again at a loss as to how to go on. He looked to Keely. She was so good at saying the right thing.

She took his silent cue. "You're right, we are getting married," she said carefully. "I know it seems sudden, maybe a little premature."

Tina snorted. "A little?"

"Neither your father nor I are the impulsive type," Keely continued, unruffled. "Under ordinary circumstances we probably would have waited awhile longer before making this decision. But there is another factor...um..." She faltered.

"What?" Tina demanded. "Are you afraid of setting a bad example for me by having sex before marriage or something dumb like that? 'Cause that's a really stupid reason to get married, just because you want to go to bed without feeling guilty that you're corrupting me. I mean, if you want to—"

"Tina," Ben interrupted before she said something even worse, "that's not the reason we're getting married." He started pacing.

"Then what? Would you just tell me?"

"I'm pregnant," Keely blurted out.

Tina's eyes bugged out and her jaw dropped. Any semblance of bored indifference melted away. "You're kidding."

Keely shook her head.

Then Tina did something that surprised the hell out of Ben. She started laughing. Ben and Keely exchanged uneasy glances.

"I'm sorry," Tina said as she struggled to control her mirth. "It's probably not funny to you guys, but don't you see the irony?"

"Irony?" Ben and Keely repeated together.

"Yeah, you know, like in my English lit class." She held up one finger and recited from memory. "Irony—a situation in which main elements are incompatible because of contrast, conflict or surprise."

"We know what it is," Ben said dryly.

Tina went on, undaunted. "Like, for years Dad's been lecturing me about waiting to have sex and not getting pregnant 'cause it would ruin my life—and you, Dr. Adams! You've talked with me about birth control and how I should look before I leap and think about the consequences of my actions, and, well, it just seems funny that the two of you got caught. Of all people!"

"We weren't careless," Ben began defensively, but he saw Keely's warning look and stopped himself. It wasn't up to him to tell anyone about her infertility.

"I'll explain it," Keely said calmly. "Tina, many years ago I was married, and we tried to have children and found out we couldn't. A doctor told me I was hopelessly infertile...that I couldn't—"

"Yeah, I know what infertile is," Tina said. As understanding dawned, the amusement melted from her face and she leaned forward, blatantly interested.

"That's why we...I didn't use birth control. The fact that I conceived a baby is like a miracle for me, although it has created a somewhat awkward situation."

To put it mildly, Ben mused.

"I don't want you to think Ben and I got 'caught,' or that we *have* to get married. There were many choices open to us. But because we care for each other, and we both believe a child should be raised by two parents, if possible, we decided marriage would be the best thing."

It occurred to Ben that Keely had described their arrangement in a very businesslike fashion. He wondered, not for the first time, if he'd done the right thing by pressuring Keely into this wedding idea.

He took a moment to study her. She stole his breath away sometimes, like now, wearing a sky blue sundress, her nose pink from the gardening she'd done this week. Her smile was sweet and radiant, especially since she'd discovered her condition. Her sensitivity toward Tina, who had offered her nothing but trouble, endeared her to him— even gave him a lump in his throat on occasion.

He did care for Keely a great deal, and he felt a certain commitment toward the unborn child. Was that enough on which to base a marriage?

"So, like, you're going to have a wedding and everything?" Tina asked, addressing Keely. "And then you're going to move in here and have a baby, right?"

"That's the gist of it," Keely said. "But I'm not trying to replace your mother. I don't plan to move in and dump a bunch of new rules on you or make you eat your spinach and clean up your room. I just hope we can learn to live together and treat each other with respect. And *maybe* we could even become friends. Someday.''

Ben gave her a look that said, *Don't push it.*

Tina sighed heavily. ''Is that it? Have you guys told me everything now?''

''That's it,'' Ben said, figuring it was hopeless to wish for a more positive response. ''You can go.''

''Oh, wait, one more thing,'' Keely said as Tina climbed off her chair. ''Would you be a bridesmaid?'' The hopeful expression on Keely's face made his heart ache. *Please, Tina, don't hurt her. She's been through so much.*

Tina looked horrified at first. Then the expression softened to a mere wrinkling of her nose. ''Would I have to wear a dress?''

''Well, yes.''

''If you make me wear something with a lot of ribbons and bows, I'll throw up,'' she warned.

''You can help me pick out the dresses,'' Keely quickly offered. ''I'm not much for ribbons and bows, either.''

Something flashed in Tina's eyes. Ben interpreted it as a look of female conspiracy. The mention of shopping must have done it.

Amazingly Tina flashed a fleeting smile before resuming her carefully constructed boredom. ''Okay, if you really want me to.'' She grabbed a second croissant and made a clean getaway this time.

Ben reclaimed his chair. Keely slumped in hers. ''I'm glad that's over,'' she said, taking a bite out of her previously untouched pastry.

''You know, the news of a baby is what won her over,'' he said. ''She was angry until you told her you were pregnant.''

"An unplanned pregnancy is something she can relate to," Keely said. "One of her close friends is going through it. She has probably wondered how she would feel in that position. I think it gave her some measure of empathy she wouldn't have had otherwise."

"You're sounding like a psychologist again," Ben teased. Then he sobered. "The battle's not over yet, is it?"

"I doubt it. Tina hasn't even begun to consider the implications. First she'll have to deal with another woman living in her house. Then she'll have a new brother or sister. For the first time in her life, she'll have to share your attention with a sibling. It's going to be a big adjustment."

"For all of us," Ben added, thinking Tina wouldn't be alone in her jealousy. He'd only just reclaimed Keely. He wasn't ready to share her with a baby.

Every time he thought about the birth of this kid, his mind froze with fear. He'd done his level best to raise Tina well. He'd given her every advantage and lots of love, and she'd ended up a juvenile delinquent. Although her behavior had improved, he still had his doubts about how she would ultimately turn out. He took personal responsibility for every setback. What could he have done differently? How could he have been a better parent?

To contemplate another twenty years of that responsibility produced a numbing terror... and yet, that's exactly what he'd committed himself to.

"You're quiet," Keely said.

He leaned toward her, brushed her cheek with his lips, then impulsively claimed her mouth with his for a more passionate kiss.

"What was that for?" she wanted to know when he released her.

"Because you're brave and beautiful, and you're the only person I've ever known who can handle my daughter. Doesn't she scare you? How can you face motherhood with so much optimism after dealing with the Teenager from Hell?"

She laughed uneasily. "Ben! What a thing to say. You forget, I've spent years dealing with children's problems. I know what I'm getting into, and I can promise you I won't change my mind. I'll even enjoy mothering that prickly daughter of yours, despite what I just told her. Now stop worrying."

She had a point. In his worst nightmare, he couldn't imagine Keely abandoning her child, as Nora had. But it wasn't inconceivable that she might someday leave Ben. What if he couldn't hack it as a father? If his convictions were wrong—if this hastily constructed family turned out to be an unhealthy environment for the child—Keely wouldn't hesitate. She would go. She would do whatever was best for her offspring, no questions asked.

Once a woman decided to leave, that was that. Nothing he'd said or did had prevented his breakup with Nora. Not that he had truly loved Nora by the time she walked out. Still, when it came to something as important as saving a marriage and holding a family together, it was scary to be so powerless.

The trick, he decided, was simply not to hope for too much. He would take things one day at a time, being very careful about how much of himself he allowed to become involved.

"I'm so glad you're here," Keely said to Eileen as she struggled into one gossamer stocking. The two sisters were up in Ben's bedroom so that Keely could dress for the wedding. "I'm such a nervous wreck, I don't know what

I'm doing. There, does that look right?'' She stood and examined the stocking in a full-length mirror on the back of the closet door.

"It looks fine, but I hope you can put the other one on in something less than fifteen minutes. You act like you've never worn stockings in your life!''

"I haven't. They'd already invented panty hose about the time I started wearing hose. This garter-belt business is new to me. I don't know how women put up with them for all those years.''

"You might not like it, but I bet Ben will,'' Eileen teased.

"I didn't buy them for Ben,'' Keely said peevishly. "I bought them because I wanted this color, and they didn't have it in panty hose.'' She cursed softly as she nicked one of her carefully polished fingernails fastening the final garter.

"I've never seen you like this,'' Eileen said, her voice full of concern as she sat on the bed next to her younger sister. "Are you worried that Mom and Dad won't get here on time?'' Keely's mother had called hours ago to report car trouble, but had promised to make the wedding one way or another.

Keely smiled wistfully at the thought of her parents. They had been so completely supportive when she'd told them what the situation was. "No, that's not it. Mom threatened to hitchhike if they couldn't get the car started. If they're late, we'll just hold up the ceremony until they get here.''

"Then what?'' Eileen persisted. "Even if something goes wrong with the wedding—which it won't—it's not the wedding that matters. It's the marriage that comes after.''

"*That's* what I'm worried about,'' Keely admitted. She hesitated, then plunged ahead, for the first time voicing the doubts that plagued her. "I don't think Ben loves me. He's trying to do the right thing for me and the baby, but I'm not sure it's the right thing for him."

"Why would you say that? Have you seen the way the man looks at you? He adores you."

"But he hasn't . . . we haven't made love since that first time. We were just getting back on track when I found out about the baby, and since then things have been crazy. He's been working twelve and fifteen hours a day while the weather holds, and trying to get Tina ready for school on top of that. I've been running around putting this wedding together. We've hardly *seen* each other the past month, let alone had time to do anything else."

"That'll change," Eileen said confidently. "Soon as he sees you in those undies."

Maybe, Keely conceded. But she couldn't put to rest the suspicion that Ben had been purposely holding himself at a distance. Even when they did reestablish an intimate relationship, there was much more to a marriage than good sex.

"I still wish we were taking a real honeymoon," she said. "One night at a fancy hotel—that's all the time he can afford to take off right now."

"So he'll make it up to you this winter—a vacation to the mountains around Christmas. Think positive."

Keely smiled despite herself. "How do you do it? How do you keep your life so happy and balanced?"

Eileen thought for a moment. "I guess with three kids, if everything's not perfect I'm too busy to worry about it. I try to enjoy the good times and just get through the rest. It's all anyone can hope for."

"Maybe I'm asking too much," Keely said glumly. It wasn't the first time the thought had crossed her mind.

"No, you're not. You have a perfect right to ask for and enjoy every bit of happiness you can find—especially on your wedding day."

A knock on the door interrupted their heart-to-heart. "Hello?" a high-pitched voice called out. "Are you in there, honey?"

"Mom!" Keely rushed to the door and flung it open, immediately swallowing her diminutive mother in a bear hug. "I'm so glad you finally made it."

"I told you your father would get us here in time," Dorothy Adams scolded. "Wild horses couldn't have kept us away."

"Did he get the car started?"

"No. We had to borrow Ernie Porter's from next door. But we're here."

"I see you got your corsage." Keely straightened the carnation she'd just knocked askew with her hug.

"Yes. A lovely young lady with, um, an innovative hairstyle gave it to me. Ben's daughter?"

Keely grimaced. "That's Tina. Yesterday she dyed the tips of her hair green, supposedly 'to match the dress.' But I know a silent protest when I see one."

"Oh, dear," Dorothy said with a clicking of her tongue. "She's not happy about the wedding?"

"Not particularly. But she is wearing a dress and behaving herself. I suppose I should be thankful she isn't carrying a protest sign or blocking the aisle. She's not really a bad kid. Not all the time, anyway."

"Well, the dress looks beautiful on her, anyway," Dorothy said. She paused to take stock of her older daughter. "It looks nice on you, too, Eileen. I never would have picked such a plain style as a bridesmaid dress, but the leaf green is very flattering. Keely, where are your clothes? It's almost time."

Keely's hands shook as she stepped into the champagne-colored silk dress. The style was straight and utterly unadorned, draping elegantly over her body to a knee-length hemline. It didn't look much like a wedding dress—no lace, beads, or ruffles. But Keely hadn't been able to pass it up.

With a dainty crown of flowers arranged in her hair, holding her bouquet, she took one last look in the mirror. She *did* look like a bride. The enormity of what she was about to do made her head spin.

The ceremony itself went by in a blur. Later she didn't remember much except for the way Ben had looked at her as she walked down the aisle in the family room. He had gazed at her with blatant approval and an expression of . . . what, wonder? Or was it panic? Her own heart had felt full to the bursting point with love. He was a good man. He would be a responsible, dutiful husband and father, despite his apprehension.

Please let him love me as well as the baby. She sent up the fervent prayer just as they joined hands to exchange vows. If only he would, theirs could be the best marriage on earth. If he didn't . . . she wasn't sure she could remain in a loveless marriage, even with an exceptionally good man.

The vows were spoken in what seemed to be seconds to Keely. She and Ben exchanged plain gold bands. The minister declared them husband and wife. Finally Ben gave her a not-quite-chaste kiss and a steamy look that made her heart flutter and her face flush, and it was all over.

Immediately she was propelled into a series of exuberant hugs from the close friends and family who had attended the small ceremony. Even Tina gave her a brief, dutiful embrace. The sense of unreality faded, and she was once again ordinary, practical Keely Adams.

Or rather, Keely Kinkaid.

A rush of champagne-drinking and cake-eating followed. Keely made a special attempt to be friendly to her new in-laws, whom she'd met today for the first time. Ben did the same with her family. They exchanged glances from across the room. Suddenly Keely wished it was all over. What had possessed her to plan a wedding, anyway? They should have eloped as Ben had wanted to do.

Her throat was dry and her toes hurt inside her stiff, high-heeled pumps. She went to the kitchen to get a glass of water. As she stood at the sink, a strong pair of hands grasped her around the waist. "Hello, stranger.

All Keely wanted to do was melt against him. It was almost as if he *were* a stranger, they'd seen so little of each other. She turned and found herself backed up against the sink, in the circle of Ben's arms. "Hello, yourself," she said a bit breathlessly. He looked big and solid and respectable in his staid gray suit, but the mischievous gleam in his green-gold eyes contradicted all the rest.

"I haven't had a chance to tell you how beautiful you look." He brushed her cheek with his knuckle. "Let's get out of here. I want you all to myself."

"We can't just leave," Keely objected weakly. "We have a house full of—"

"The hell we can't. It's our wedding. No one expects us to stay and empty ashtrays. My parents promised to take care of all that."

"Hmm, when you put it that way..." She flashed him a relieved smile as she tried to slip out of his arms. "I'll go change."

He held her fast. "Are you sure you want to change? I haven't fully appreciated your wedding dress." He ran his hand slowly over the smooth silk, down her body from shoulder to hip. His touch heated her blood. "I do believe, Mrs. Kinkaid, that your curves are just a bit more lush than they were a month ago."

"Oh, don't remind me," Keely groaned. "I've already gained six pounds and I'm barely three months along. I'm retaining liquids like a water buffalo, and I'm going to look like one before too long."

Ben laughed and kissed her gently on the mouth. "You'll make a beautiful water buffalo. Oh, go on, change your clothes if you have to," he said, releasing his hold on her. "I'm sure you have a 'going-away' outfit you're dying to show off. But hurry up. I've had about all the hugs from my aunt Celia that I can take. And I have a surprise for you."

Keely escaped before she gave in to temptation and stole another kiss. She felt immeasurably cheered by Ben's ardor. She'd been half-afraid that he wouldn't desire her body anymore, now that she was pregnant. Pregnancy was so... *matronly*.

She slipped up to the bedroom by herself, needing some time alone. She took off the dress and hung it in a plastic bag. She removed the flowers from her hair and laid them on the dresser, then carefully took stock of her image in the mirror.

Already she looked different. For the first time in her life she had a bustline inching toward voluptuous, and her waist had thickened. She liked the new, riper Keely, she decided, but she knew she'd better enjoy it while she could. Before long she would be far past ripe.

Would Ben still look at her with that gleam in his eye? Or would he find her hugeness distasteful? If they didn't have at least *that* going for them, what would happen to their marriage?

She forced herself to put aside her doubts. For tonight, at least, she had her husband's full attention. She was going to take every advantage.

She had planned to change out of the frivolous garter belt and stockings, but when she remembered what Eileen had said about how Ben would appreciate the sexy lingerie, she left them on. She quickly stepped into a mint green skirt and pulled a white silk shell over her head. So what if the stockings didn't match the rest of the outfit?

Nine

Keely stretched and kicked off her shoes, giving a loud, satisfied sigh. She was seated on the passenger side of Ben's Porsche, relaxed for the first time in what seemed years. They'd finally managed to extricate themselves from the wedding reception and make their escape.

She curled her stocking feet under her for the short drive downtown. At least, she *thought* that's where they were heading. But Ben didn't take the downtown exit. Instead, he turned the car east on I-70. "Where are you going?" she asked. "I thought our reservations were at the Allis Plaza."

"They were," Ben said with a smug smile. "I changed them."

"To where?"

"A bed-and-breakfast at Lake of the Ozarks. I hope you don't mind the drive."

"Mind the drive?" she repeated in a voice that was almost a squeal of delight. "Of course not. But . . . why?"

"Because you looked so sad when I told you I couldn't take time off for more than a night downtown. I felt like the biggest heel. What kind of a jerk lets business get in the way of a honeymoon? You went to a lot of trouble to make the wedding special even after I'd pushed you into getting married—"

"You didn't push me," she interjected. "And I didn't mean to send you on a guilt trip."

"Yes, I did push you. Anyway, I figured the least I could do was make some kind of an effort toward a reasonable facsimile of a honeymoon. So yesterday I went to a travel agent and she suggested this place. I reserved a room for three nights. It's not much, I know, but—"

"Three nights. That'll be heaven!" Impulsively she unfastened her seat belt, leaned over and threw her arms around his neck, planting a noisy kiss on his cheek.

Ben laughed and struggled to see around her arm. He'd been hoping she would feel this way. "You like the idea?"

"I love it. Oh, Ben, we need to get reacquainted. We've hardly seen each other. I don't want to be married to a stranger."

Her words touched him. Was that really how she felt? He admitted he'd been holding back with her, struggling to get a grip on his own feelings regarding the sudden turn his life had taken before he got himself in so deep he couldn't see daylight. But he'd never meant to be a stranger to her.

"How was your checkup with Dr. McCommas?" he asked.

Her only reaction to the abrupt change of subject was a curious, sideways glance. "Fine. I'm a little anemic, and I have to watch my diet because I'm retaining water and my blood sugar is a little too high, but—"

"Really? Why didn't you tell me this?" he asked sharply.

"You didn't ask." He couldn't miss the note of hurt in her voice. "Anyway, it's nothing to worry about. I'm just experiencing the same symptoms lots of pregnant women have. Pat said everything else looks fine, and if I'll just take care of myself, I shouldn't expect any major problems."

Ben felt like some slimy invertebrate for not showing more concern for her condition. Although he thought often about Keely and worried about her, he hadn't expressed it. He knew lots of women had babies in their mid-thirties and beyond, but he also knew there were increased risks. "What about exercise?" he asked.

"Whatever I feel like doing is okay. Of course, I haven't been to the gym in weeks. No wonder I gained six pounds."

He took her hand and laced his fingers with hers. "So what do you feel like doing? Are you up to sharing a little exercise with me?"

"Yes, of course. Some long walks would be nice. Maybe some swimming. I'm awfully tired, though. For tonight, at least, I'd like to relax."

"Oh."

After a long pause, Keely closed her eyes and hid her face in her hands. "I'm such an idiot," she said in a muffled voice. "Walking and swimming weren't the types of exercise you had in mind."

"Well..."

She looked up again. "Oh, Ben, of *course* I'll feel like making love! Wherever did you get the idea that I might not?"

He shrugged uncomfortably. "I just thought, with your delicate condition, it might not be good for you." He didn't tell her that Nora had given him the idea. After she'd found out she was pregnant with Tina she'd wanted nothing to do with sex.

"Rest assured, that is *not* the case. I am not, and never will be, delicate. How long does it take to get to this place, anyway?" she asked with a mischievous grin.

Damn. It was all he could do not to pull over to the side of the road and ravish her on the spot. He felt a pleasant tightness in his loins that grew progressively less pleasant as the Porsche ate up the miles toward the lake.

After several wrong turns, they found Taylor's Inn at the end of a winding dirt road in the small town of Rocky Mount, on Lake of the Ozarks' north shore.

"It looks so peaceful," Keely commented with obvious approval as they pulled into a barely paved parking lot.

Ben had to agree—it was just what he'd hoped for. The big, whitewashed house, while not fancy on the outside, looked cool and inviting. It sat perched on the edge of a precipice, surrounded by woods. Ben could just see the side of a vast back porch that looked out over a quiet lake channel.

They both got out of the car and drank in the country air. Ben wondered how he'd even considered shortchanging Keely or himself out of a wedding trip. The look of delight and anticipation on Keely's face was ample reward for the trouble he'd gone to to rearrange his schedule.

He opened the trunk to get their bags. "What's this?" he asked Keely, pointing inside the compartment to a large box wrapped in plain white paper.

"Oh, um, that's your wedding present from me. I meant to give it to you earlier, but there never was time, so I had Eileen sneak it in there after you'd put the bags in."

"You didn't have to get me a present," he said as he hefted the heavy box. "I didn't get you anything."

"Yes, you did," Keely argued, gesturing toward the grand old house. "You're giving it to me right now." She grabbed one of the bags from the trunk, scoffing at his objections that she shouldn't overexert.

Inside, Taylor's Inn was fancier than the outside would suggest. The elaborate Victorian decor featured dark wood floors covered with thick Persian rugs, busy floral wallpaper, overstuffed furniture, and bric-a-brac spilling across every surface. The effect was one of cheerful confusion.

"Yours is the Iris Room, to the top of the stairs and down the hall to the end," the elderly lady innkeeper told them. "Tonight we're serving chicken-fried steak with all the trimmings for dinner. If you'd like to dine here, we seat guests at six-thirty and eight-thirty."

"Put us down for the second seating," Ben said as he signed the register. Keely gave him an approving nod. That would give them several hours to "get reacquainted," as she had phrased it, and he intended to use every minute of that time to convince Keely she hadn't made a mistake by marrying him. He took the steps two at a time.

The Iris Room was a study of blue and yellow, a continuation of the fussy, romantic decor from downstairs. A series of watercolor paintings of irises hung on one wall. Cheerful floral-print drapes cascaded in ruffles and flounces down the windows. But the massive four-poster bed, heaped with all manner of pillows featuring lace, ruffles and ribbons, was the focal point of the room.

"Wow," Keely said in an awestruck voice. "I've never seen anything so romantic."

Ben thought the bed was interesting, but his attention was more keenly focused on his bride. He decided *she* was the most romantic thing *he'd* ever seen. "The only improvement I'd like to make to that bed," he said deliberately, "is to put you and me in it."

He set his bag and the heavy box on the floor, then turned toward Keely, intent on making her his.

She returned his gaze with an expectant smile, her blue eyes shining with a light of their own. "Will you open your present now?"

Now? Ben stifled an impatient sigh. The last thing he was concerned with right now was wrestling with wrapping paper and packing tape. But if that's what she wanted, he'd open the damn thing.

He picked up the box and set it on an ornately carved, cherry-wood table, then tore into the paper. Thankfully there wasn't any packing tape. He pulled open the box flaps. Inside a nest of newspaper he found an antique mantel clock—exactly the kind he'd been looking for that day he and Keely had spent in St. Joseph.

"Where did you find this?" he asked as he gingerly lifted the prize out of its box and set it on the table.

"It was in my parents' attic. I found it that weekend I went down there. I refinished the cabinet, but I'm afraid the mechanism needs some work."

"Don't worry about that," he said, unable to take his eyes off the clock. He admired the fact that she'd gone to so much trouble to give him something he really wanted. "I can probably fix it. Keely, are you sure you want to give it to me? It's a valuable piece, a family heirloom."

"And I'm keeping it in the family," she scolded. "Or have you already forgotten we're married?"

He could have bitten his tongue out for saying something so thoughtless. When would he learn? "Oh, no, I haven't forgotten. Thank you for the present. And I'll try to be a credit to your family." He took both of her hands in his, squeezed them briefly, then ran his fingertips up her bare arms, across her silk-covered shoulders, and up her neck. Finally he framed her face in his hands and slowly lowered his mouth to hers.

He kissed her with infinite tenderness, gently exploring the contours of her soft lips. She opened her mouth to his tongue, and he plumbed the warm, inviting depths. He made the kiss everything it could be—an invitation, a plea and ultimately a brand of possession.

He remembered how shy she'd been that first time, and he struggled for control. They would have only one wedding night. He wanted everything to be perfect, for both of them. Certainly he didn't want to overwhelm her with the strength of his desire.

With some effort he ended the kiss and simply held her close for several heartbeats. "Would you be offended," he murmured in her ear, "if I wanted to assert my conjugal rights, right now, before dinner, in broad daylight?"

Keely gave a low laugh. "I would be highly disappointed if you didn't." She raked his back suggestively with her fingernails, then boldly placed her hands on his buttocks. "I'm not sure anything could match our first time, but I'd like to try."

Her words were unbelievably arousing. "Anything you say." He grasped her around the waist and lifted her onto the high bed, where she sat primly, looking surprised but waiting for his next move.

He gazed at her the way a student of violin looks on a Stradivarius. He wanted to play her like a virtuoso, to produce every possible beautiful note of pleasure from her body. He started by removing her shoes and stroking her stocking feet one at a time.

She fairly purred her approval as the sensual massage moved up first one calf, then the other. He liked the smooth, slippery feel of her stockings, but he preferred the silk of bare skin.

His hands wandered above her knees, a leisurely exploration. They crept under the hem of her skirt, moving in lazy circles. All the while he watched her eyes, enjoying the response he saw in them. Her pupils dilated and the blue brightness of her irises darkened. His hands gradually moved up her legs. Her breathing came faster.

When he found the tops of her stockings and the satiny garter straps, he gave a surprised gasp of his own. In his wilder imaginings he had often pictured Keely's beautiful body wrapped in sexy lingerie, but he hadn't expected to see it without some prompting on his part.

She laughed and looked down at her lap, obviously embarrassed. "I wore them for you."

"In that case, I'd like to get the full effect." He picked her up as easily as he would a doll and stood her up next to the bed. Without ever letting her go, he slid his hands over her rib cage and to the back of her skirt, where the fastening was. "You don't mind, do you?"

"No." Her voice was soft; he could feel the warmth of her breath against his neck.

The skirt fell to the floor with a whisper. She kicked it aside. Her lacy half-slip followed. With a bit of encouragement, she peeled her blouse over her head and tossed it over an overstuffed chair. In just her bra, panties and those erotic stockings and garter belt, she thrust back her shoulders and met his eyes boldly. She held that pose for all of three seconds before laughing and looking at anything but him. Her whole body blushed to a rosy hue.

"I once told you, you're going to have to get used to me staring at you," he said as he took two steps backward in order to more fully admire her. "You look . . . perfect."

"Perfectly ridiculous," she amended. "I'm not sure I'm the type to wear this stuff."

"You are. Trust me." Ben's voice was husky with desire. He wanted Keely as he'd never wanted any woman. She reflected all the wantonness of a practiced temptress combined with the modesty and purity of a virgin. The new contours of her body excited him. She was Eve, the first woman, temptation embodied. She was an earth goddess, an icon of fertility. He'd known for a month now that she carried his child, but he'd never thought the fact *sexy* until now.

"Is there a sign on me that says, Look But Don't Touch?" she asked playfully, her sense of boldness returning.

He held out his hand to her and she grasped it. "I intend to do both," he said as he pulled her toward him and wrapped his arms around her.

"So do I." She tugged the hem of his white golf shirt free of his slacks, then slid her hands beneath the fabric to caress the bare skin of his back. Her hands were warm. All of her was warm. He couldn't wait to feel all of her against all of him.

With her dubious help he shed his clothes, although every time she touched him in an effort to speed things along he found himself delaying so he could touch her in return. Finally, however, he was free of all restrictions. He stood back, letting her study him as he'd done her. He wanted her to know just exactly what she did to him.

Without words, she understood what he wished her to do. She went to him, put her arms around him and rubbed her body against his as if she were an affection-starved cat.

All the while, she gently scored his back with her fingernails, raking from shoulder to hip and back, making him shiver with anticipation.

She'd been timid and demure their first time together, unsure of herself, looking to him for guidance. This afternoon was a different story. Now that she'd gotten over her initial unease over being stared at, Keely was a mature woman who was sure of what she wanted. Ben was less a teacher and more the student this time.

She was the one who led them to the bed. She hopped up on the high mattress, giving him an engaging view of her bottom. With her luminous eyes she invited him to join her. He reclined on his side across the bed and leaned up on one elbow, devouring her with his eyes as she rolled the stockings down her silky legs one inspiring inch at a time.

Keely, a wanton. He was going happily crazy.

When he couldn't stand her teasing a moment longer he reached for her, pulling her against him none too gently. Apparently she had hoped for that sort of uncontrolled response from him, because her face registered definite satisfaction just before he claimed a demanding kiss.

He drank from her as if she offered the nectar of life. At that moment he felt that he needed her more desperately than he needed air to breathe. How had he stayed away from her for so long?

He ruffled her neat cap of hair with frantic fingers until it practically stood on end. He couldn't get enough of her. He wanted to inhale her, consume her, and make her as crazy with desire as he was.

Though he was sorely tempted to put an end to his own delicious pain, he instead devoted himself to studying Keely's body, finding its secrets, rediscovering what pleased her.

Her nipples strained against the confinement of her sheer bra. He teased them through the slick fabric until she moaned and yanked the thing off, throwing it aside with abandon.

He had always thought her breasts beautiful, but they were even more pleasing now, fuller, reminding him again that she carried his child. He lowered his mouth to kiss one hard, nut brown peak. At the same time he ran his palm in a gentle circle over her abdomen.

She allowed him to explore, rewarding him with sighs and soft words of encouragement. But she wasn't content to remain passive for long. Her hands began to wander over his body until, thoroughly distracted, he let her have her way with him.

The way she expressed her own passion surprised him. She was daring and innovative, showing no hesitation as she charted the territory of his body. She kissed and touched his ears, his neck, his chest, sometimes pressing hard, sometimes caressing as softly as a breeze. She seemed to be carefully noting what made him gasp with pleasure.

She moved lower, devoting herself to his rippled abdomen, tracing his tan lines with her tongue, then lower still. Her delicate fingers danced through the soft hair that surrounded his manhood. It was all he could do not to writhe with the exquisite sensations that coursed from his toes to his scalp. Never had any woman explored him so thoroughly.

Ben had to physically restrain Keely from moving on to the next logical step. If she had taken him into her mouth he would have either exploded or died trying to hold back.

Her big eyes were full of questions as she looked at him. "You don't want me to do that?"

Whatever part of his brain that formed words had short-circuited, but he did manage to shake his head.

"Too aggressive, is that it?" Her brows drew together in a worried frown, her front teeth nibbling at her lower lip.

Again he shook his head. "T-too turned on," he managed. He pulled her to him, pressing her hips against his rigid arousal as he buried his face in her soft hair. His control was still tenuous at best. "You're driving me crazy. Let me make love to you."

"Oh, yes, I'd like that."

So polite, he mused as he watched her slide her white lace panties down her legs. As if she were accepting an invitation to tea. Yet there was no artifice in it. She just did what came naturally, becoming a devilish temptress one minute, a sweet angel the next. It was a potent combination.

She gave him a sexy half smile of invitation as she lay on her back, legs primly closed, waiting for him to do with her as he pleased. The trust she showed moved him.

He smiled back tenderly. Sex had always been a satisfying experience for him, something he looked forward to. But never had it been such a joyful occasion, involving his heart as well as his body. She filled his loins with an unbearable tightness, but she also filled his chest, his heart, the seat of his soul.

An errant sunbeam illuminated a slanted path across her body. He traced it with his finger, across her breast, her ribs, her stomach and through the nest of dark curls that protected the secrets of her femininity. With the same light caressing motion he tickled her thighs, insinuating his hand between them, urging them open.

It didn't take much urging. She was as ready to accept him as he was to be inside her. Still a bit wary of her condition, he eased his body on top of hers, watching where his weight fell. He imagined himself a brook, flowing gently over her body the way water streams over stones.

"I'm not going to break." She bent her knees up on either side of his hips, opening herself to him, making it oh-so-easy to bury himself in her depths. Still, he entered her as slowly as he could manage, wanting to draw out the pleasure.

She made a sound, a low growl in the back of her throat, reminding him of the tigress she could be. She curled her feet around his calves and pulled him closer until they truly were one.

He couldn't stop touching her. As they rocked back and forth, driven by passion, he filled his hands with her, running them through her soft hair, over her face, cupping her breasts. Their intimate dance suggested a union of spirit as well as bodies. She was his. They had promised to each other through eternity, and at that moment he thought maybe they'd reached the infinite.

He forgot all about holding any part of himself back from Keely.

Release came swiftly, violently. He cried out and tossed his head like a horse. She gripped him with hands surprisingly strong as her body was racked with tremors. He was almost out of his mind with ecstasy, but not so far gone that he didn't see the single tear that seeped from the corner of her eye as she found her release.

His lovemaking had never moved a woman to tears before. As with the first time with Keely, he had found a new dimension in the physical act of loving, an act that had once been familiar to him. Now he was finding intimacy to be a brand-new experience. He couldn't wait to learn more.

They lay together in contented silence. Keely slowly became aware of her surroundings—the idle ceiling fan above her, the quilted bedspread under her back and all those lacy, ruffly, beribboned pillows scattered around them. It seemed funny, she and Ben lying naked and sweaty and deliciously carnal among those pillows, those symbols of sweet Victorian romance.

"What are you laughing at?" Ben asked, rolling over and pulling her on top of him.

"All these silly little pillows. We've mussed them up."

"And how." He smiled the smile of a satisfied man.

Keely stood by the window and stared out at the still, moonlit water. Ben lay in a deep sleep on the four-poster bed a few feet away. It was late—probably two or three o'clock in the morning, she judged—but she couldn't sleep.

This was their third night at Taylor's Inn. Although brief, their honeymoon had been almost everything Keely could have wanted. They had taken those long walks she'd promised, and had gone swimming and sailing on the lake. They had eaten some wonderful meals, both here and at a few of the lake's four-star restaurants. They had spent one hilarious afternoon on the Bagnell strip, a mecca for tacky tourist attractions, shopping, having their pictures made, sipping on cool fresh-squeezed lemonade.

And they had spent hours in bed. More times than Keely could count they had mussed up those pillows, sometimes knocking them off the bed or sending them flying across the room.

Only one thing was missing. Ben had never come close to telling her he loved her. Sometimes she thought she sensed it, when their bodies were joined. That's when she felt closest to him. But at all other times, though they laughed and teased and got along famously, Ben revealed little of his inner feelings.

Several times she had almost said the words herself. But always she stopped herself. She couldn't bear to press him, then find out he really didn't love her, or that he never would. If that was the case, she wanted to hold on to her blissful ignorance awhile longer.

She wished she had more time in this wonderful place. But in a few hours they would be leaving all this behind, returning to the real world. If only they could hold onto the mood of young, carefree lovers, she thought, genuine love might follow. But that was impossible. Life's harsh realities were bound to interfere with the tenuous bonds of marriage forming between them.

Ten

Outside the snow was piling up, but inside the Kinkaid home it was warm and cozy. A few minutes ago Keely had put a pan of enchiladas into the oven, and now the kitchen was awash with the tempting scent of baking corn tortillas, cheese and spicy sauce.

Cooking had never been a priority in Keely's life. Over the past four months, however, she had discovered she liked preparing meals for more than one. She had spent many hours poring over cookbooks and magazines, searching out the recipes she thought Ben and Tina would like and sometimes experimenting with her own concoctions. Enchiladas had become a favorite with the whole family, which was why she'd decided to make them tonight. After the disaster at school today, she needed to create a positive atmosphere at home.

Keely leaned down to get place mats from a lower cabinet and almost toppled over. She still wasn't used to her new weight distribution. Over the past month she had suddenly "blossomed," so that now she looked as if she'd swallowed a basketball. Everyone who saw her assumed she was full-term, and she still had seven weeks to go. She couldn't imagine what size she would be by the time she gave birth. Would she even fit into a car so she could get to the hospital?

She groaned as she straightened, place mats in hand. Suddenly she was exhausted. The things she used to take in stride—working all day, then coming home to clean and cook—wore her to a frazzle now that her figure resembled Jumbo the Elephant's. Her hands and feet were swollen and her back ached constantly. She also found it difficult to sleep. She used to sleep on her stomach, but that was no longer possible.

As Keely finished setting the table, the front door opened and Tina breezed in, bringing a cold gust of air with her. She trailed snow all the way into the kitchen as she divested herself of her winter gear.

"Hi, Keely," she said cheerfully, hopping on one foot as she pulled her boot off the other. "Did you hear about what happened to Annie Parker?"

"Yes. Unfortunately I was right in the middle of it."

"Was she a client of yours?"

"Now you know I can't talk about that."

"It was cool, all those sirens, and the fire truck and the paramedics. We were supposed to be taking a math test but it got all disrupted and everyone was running to the windows and looking down the hall, and half the kids started cheating."

Keely slammed down a handful of silverware. "Tina, it was *not* cool. That girl tried to take her own life. You could at least show a little sensitivity."

Tina waved away Keely's concern. "She wasn't really trying to kill herself. She took a handful of pills and then immediately told everyone about it so they'd get her to the hospital. She just wanted attention."

"Thank you, Dr. Tina, for that diagnosis," Keely said dryly. Annie Parker had been her client for two years. Keely had known Annie was a very troubled girl, but the suicide attempt had come as a complete shock. She couldn't help but feel guilty for not doing something to prevent it—and angry at Tina for her lack of compassion. "Dinner will be in about fifteen minutes," she said quietly, deciding a change of subject was in order before she really lost her temper.

"I'm not hungry," Tina said on her way out of the kitchen.

"What?" Keely heard herself almost screeching.

Tina turned, appearing confused at the sudden outburst. "Someone brought in a pizza at work, so I'm not hungry."

Keely sighed with exasperation. "Could you at least sit at the table with us?"

Tina rolled her eyes. "I have homework to do." With that she made a fast exit.

Keely wasn't done with the conversation. She followed Tina toward her room, talking the whole way. "Look, Tina, I went to some trouble to fix a special dinner tonight. You could have called and let me know you didn't want to eat at home. Failing that, you could at least—"

Tina turned abruptly, blocking the door to her room. "Jeez, Keely, would you give it a rest? I've eaten dinner at home every night this week. I've had it up to *here* with family togetherness. You're trying too hard. You run around cooking and cleaning and decorating—my God, the Christmas decorations! You went nuts! It's like you're trying to fix something when it's not broken. There was nothing wrong with this house before you came, and there's nothing wrong with it now except you're driving everybody crazy trying to make us into the perfect family."

Keely started to object, but Tina wasn't finished.

"We're not the perfect family, so stop playing Donna Reed. If you would just relax—"

"You've made your point," Keely snapped. She whirled around and stalked away before Tina could see the tears in her eyes. She heard the bedroom door slam behind her.

She went back to the kitchen table and slumped into one of the chairs, sniffing back her tears. This was the first time she had fought with Tina in a long time. Keely had thought things were going so well, but now it appeared that beneath the surface, a lot of resentment seethed.

Maybe Tina was right. Maybe Keely *was* trying too hard to be the perfect wife—to make up for the fact that Ben had been drawn into a marriage and a new family situation he hadn't asked for and didn't really want.

That thought made her empty stomach clench into a painful knot. Dammit, if the two of them didn't appreciate the efforts she made to please them, why hadn't they said something sooner? She could only assume Ben shared Tina's feelings. The tension in this house was almost palpable. Keely had tried to sweep it under the carpet, but it was time to admit that everything wasn't as it should be.

She checked the enchiladas. Another five minutes. She hoped Ben made it home soon. The snow had probably slowed him down, but it was well past seven. Where could he be?

As if in answer to her silent question, the phone rang. Her muscles protested as she stood and closed the oven door. She started toward the phone—slowly—but it stopped ringing before she could get to it. A minute or so later, Tina yelled up the basement stairs that the call was for Keely.

"Hi, honey," Ben greeted her, his voice full of blatant concern. "Tina tells me you're a little upset. Are you all right?"

"I'm fine," she said dismissively, resisting the urge to blame Tina for *causing* the upset. "Just a bad day at school, and that made me a little short with Tina. It'll be okay." She wished she could believe that herself. "Where are you?"

"At a pay phone. It looks like I won't make it home for dinner."

"Why not?" Again Keely winced at the shrillness of her own voice. It was almost as if she couldn't control it.

"I slid my car into a ditch," he answered with obvious disgust. "The tow truck won't be here for—"

"Are you okay? Was anyone hurt?"

"No one was hurt. Even the car's okay, but it's stuck."

Keely tried to tell herself that this wasn't a catastrophe. So, her dinner was ruined. Ben certainly hadn't driven his car into a ditch on purpose just to make her bad day worse. Nonetheless, her throat clogged with a silent sob. "When will you be home?"

"What? I can't hear you. The traffic..."

She repeated her question, more forcefully this time.

"I don't know. Late, it looks like. Go ahead and eat without me. Um, what am I missing?"

"Enchiladas."

He groaned melodramatically. "Save me some. I'll heat 'em up when I get home."

"No. I plan to eat the whole panful myself and get even fatter."

"What? I'm sorry, honey, I couldn't hear you. The traffic—"

"It was nothing."

"Keely? Are you sure you're okay?"

"Yeah. I'll see you when you get home." She hung up and dissolved into a wretched, self-pitying puddle of tears.

It was about nine o'clock by the time Ben finally made it home. His stomach was growling, and he'd thought briefly about stopping for fast food on the way home, then had nixed the idea. He'd better eat Keely's enchiladas and vigorously enjoy them. Keely had given him the idea that she wasn't too pleased with him, although she'd done nothing outwardly to indicate that.

The house was dark as he came through the front door. Had Keely already gone to bed? Although he knew she needed the extra rest, he selfishly hoped she was still awake. He enjoyed sharing his day with her and listening to hers. Sometimes the baby kicked while they talked. She claimed it responded to his voice.

He started upstairs toward the bedroom, then paused as a noxious, burning smell registered. Thinking perhaps Keely had left the oven on—although that wasn't like her—he went to the kitchen to check. As soon as he turned the light on he saw the source of the odor, sitting on the counter—one pan of enchiladas, burned to a black brick.

"Poor Keely," he murmured as he set the pan in the sink and ran water over it. Her bad day had gotten even worse.

He was about to turn off the kitchen light when he heard a peculiar noise from the family room. At first he thought it was just wind whistling through the chimney. Then he heard it again and realized it was the sound of sobbing.

"Keely?"

"Don't turn on the light," she said just as he reached for the switch. "I'm fat and ugly and my face is all red and blotchy and I don't want you to see me."

"You are *not* fat," he insisted. "I believe the politically correct term is, 'reproductively challenged.'" His joke didn't produce even a snicker. He gave up on the light switch and sat down next to Keely in the dark. When he tried to put his arm around her, her shoulders were stiff and unyielding. "Honey, what's wrong?"

"Aside from the fact that one of my clients tried to kill herself, Tina and I had a big fight and I burned the dinner nobody wanted anyway? Not a thing."

"Oh, honey. I'm . . . I'm sorry." He felt totally inadequate at this comforting stuff. Keely was usually strong and stoic about her problems and not prone to feeling sorry for herself. She had seldom needed comforting. Still, he had to make a stab at it. "I know you think of your clients as family, and it's hard when one of them goes astray, but you can't hold yourself responsible."

"That's what everyone keeps telling me." Her voice was flat.

"As for Tina," Ben continued, "this is the first real argument you've had in months. That's a pretty good track record. I wouldn't worry about it. Sometimes she just gets in the mood to fight, and she fights tough."

Keely made no response to that.

"As for dinner, *I* wanted your enchiladas."

"Then why didn't you get home at a reasonable hour?" A new batch of tears accompanied the demand.

"I told you," he explained patiently, "my car went into a ditch—"

"I know, I know. Don't even listen to me. I'm totally irrational. I wish I could blame it on hormones, but that's a cheap cop-out."

"It probably *is* your hormones," Ben said. "What did you and Tina argue about?"

"She says I overdecorated for Christmas."

"What? What does that have to do with anything?"

"Then you agree?"

"Well..." He struggled furiously to come up with the right answer. "We've never done much decorating in the past, so it was kind of a shock to come home to a twelve-foot tree and pine boughs and wreaths and angels all over the place, but—"

"So Tina was right."

"About what? I still don't understand—"

"She thinks I'm trying too hard, that I'm driving the both of you crazy with my exaggerated efforts to make this a happy home. In short, she thinks everything was better before I came along and started forcing all my sinister family ways on the two of you."

"Did she say that?" He found that difficult to believe. Tina's attitude toward Keely was wonderfully positive most of the time. Once she had even admitted in a whisper that she was glad he had married Keely.

"Not in those words, but that's what she meant."

"I'm sure you're mistaken."

"I'm not. I'm a psychologist, trained to read between the lines."

"You're also much too close to this situation to be objective, and you know it." He removed his arm from around her shoulders since she was having none of his comforting anyway. "Did you eat dinner?"

She shook her head.

"Want me to fix you a sandwich?"

"I'm not hungry."

"Maybe you aren't, but I'll bet the baby is. He'll be kicking you all night if you don't feed him."

She said nothing.

"Well, I'll make sandwiches for both of us. You don't have to eat yours if you don't want to." He got up and went to the kitchen. Her silence worried him. He'd been witness to her hormonal swings before—all perfectly normal for a pregnant woman, according to her doctor. Sometimes his practical, down-to-earth Keely ranted and raved in perfect illogic. He had learned not to take offense. But this quiet sadness was new.

Because the kitchen and family room were separated only by a work island, he continued to talk as he slapped together a couple of turkey sandwiches. "I think I know what Tina was getting at."

"Oh?"

"You're working too hard. You put in a full day at school, and then you come home and work another eight-hour shift here. It's not good for you, especially in your condition. I can tell you're worn-out." Lately she'd been sporting dark circles under her eyes, but he prudently decided not to point that out, as sensitive as she was about her appearance. He thought she was beautiful no matter what her size, but she found that hard to believe.

"I like doing things for you," she objected.

"And I appreciate it. But why not let Tina and me take care of you for a while? We can cook and do laundry and run the sweeper just as easily as you can." He set her sandwich on the coffee table in front of her, then sat in a chair opposite and began devouring his.

"If I waited for you and Tina to fix dinner and do laundry, we would all die of starvation—wearing dirty clothes."

"That is not true," he said between bites. "How do you think we survived before you came here? I was a pretty good housekeeper and cook, even if I do say so myself."

"Only because you had to. Now you have me."

"I didn't marry you so you could run yourself into the ground being Suzy Homemaker."

"We both know perfectly well why you married me. Let's not even bring that into the discussion."

Oh, hell. He took another large bite of his sandwich and chewed it thoroughly to prevent himself from saying something he'd regret. There was no getting around the fact that he had married her because she was pregnant, but he seldom thought about his reasons anymore. So far, he was enjoying married life. Keely, on the other hand, couldn't seem to let go of the reasons. Sometimes he got the distinct impression that she thought she had to somehow "make it up to him." She *did* try too hard, as his tactless daughter had so thoughtlessly informed her.

"Keely, I've been thinking about something, and now's as good a time as any to bring it up."

"What?" she asked suspiciously.

"I think you should go away for a while."

"What?"

"Now hear me out before you get bent out of shape. You need some rest, and it's obvious you aren't going to get any here. Go stay with your parents—or your sister. Hasn't she been bugging you to visit? You could put your feet up, watch TV and read, take all the naps you want—"

"No."

"No? Just like that? You won't even think about it?"

"I will not let you send me away like . . . like some overgrown pet that's gotten to be too much trouble."

"That is *not* why I want you to go. Dammit, Keely, I don't *want* you to go, but I'm worried about you. I'm concerned for your health as well as the baby's. Can't you see that?"

"What I see is a man who wants to send his wife away," she said, just short of hysterical. "You want things back the way they were before I came here. Then, after I've been gone a little while, it'll be easier to make the separation permanent. Well, I won't let you off that easy. I'm staying right here. If you want a divorce, you'll have to look me in the eye and ask for one."

A divorce? Where did she get this stuff? The woman was out of her mind. "Keely," he said wearily, "try as I might, I can't follow your logic tonight. This discussion has gotten completely out of control. Before it gets any worse, I'm going to bed. I can only hope you will have regained your senses by morning." He took his empty plate and headed for the kitchen.

Before he took too many steps, he paused, noticing her untouched sandwich. "Do you want a glass of milk with that or something?" he asked, gesturing toward her plate.

She shook her head.

With many regrets, he went up to the bedroom alone and left Keely to brood in the dark. What else could he do? She was determined to twist everything he said and believe the worst. Under those circumstances, he couldn't win.

In a way, though, he was selfishly glad she hadn't snapped up his suggestion that she go away. Although a restful vacation would be good for her, he didn't like the idea of being separated from her. In her present state of mind, it would be all too easy for her to convince herself that she was better off without him. Now, at least, he knew she was determined to stay with him until they'd either worked out their problems or...the "or" didn't bear thinking about.

Funny, until tonight he hadn't believed they had any problems. But Keely had forced him to look at things from a different angle. With all her frantic efforts to build a homey little nest for her new family, maybe she was trying to convince *herself* that she hadn't made a grave mistake.

Downstairs, the mantel clock, Keely's wedding present to Ben, chimed ten. Keely knew she should go to bed. Nothing was accomplished by sitting here alone, going over and over what she'd said, what he'd said and what shouldn't have been said at all.

He was right. She'd lost her mind, or at least she'd behaved as if she had. What was wrong with her? Ben had tried to comfort her. He would have done *anything* to make her feel better. And she'd attacked him at every turn, reading evil intentions behind his words. She could only blame so much on hormones.

Deep down, she knew he had her welfare at heart. He was nothing if not duty-bound to care for her and the baby, so he wouldn't send her away out of pure selfishness. Still, she had no idea what he wanted for himself. If only for one minute he would be honest with her about his own needs, his own feelings.

No matter how good his intentions, though, she planned to stay right here and deal with whatever came up. She would keep this family together or die trying.

One week later, the stern look on Pat McCommas's face threatened Keely's good intentions. The doctor didn't appear the least bit encouraging.

"Well?" Keely asked from her undignified position on a gurney in a treatment bay at the emergency room. She had slipped on the ice and taken a hard fall in the parking lot at school. Naturally there had been no one around to help her. Somehow she had maneuvered to her feet, intending to drive straight home and climb into bed. A series of sharp pains had changed her plans, and she'd headed for the ER instead.

"Do you want me to sugarcoat it, or give it to you straight?"

"Oh, God, there's nothing wrong with the baby, is there?"

"No, by all my calculations, the kid's as healthy as a horse."

"He certainly kicks like one," Keely muttered.

"You, on the other hand, are a mess. You're anemic, borderline diabetic and on the ragged edge of exhaustion. I've been warning you for months that you needed to take better care of yourself—"

"I know."

"You shouldn't have gone back to work after the Christmas break."

"Friday's my last day, I swear."

"No. Today was your last day. You could have easily gone into labor this afternoon and given birth six weeks early. Is that what you want?"

"Of course not," Keely said meekly.

"Granted, these days we can save most preemies born past seven months, but do you want to take that risk?"

"Pat, you know I don't."

"Then pay attention. Bottom line is, I want you flat on your back until this kid makes an appearance. That means *in bed*, in your jammies. No cooking, no cleaning, no running outside to get the paper."

"But how can I—" Keely cut herself off. Pat was serious this time.

"Find a relative to stay with you—how about your mother? Or you could hire a nurse."

Keely could just see that—bringing in another stranger to an already tense household. "If you want me to reduce the stress in my life, that's not the answer."

"All right, then you go stay with someone."

Initially Keely bristled at that suggestion. "I can't just leave Ben and..." Her voice trailed off as Pat continued to stare with that accusatory gleam in her eye. She was making Keely feel like an unfit mother-to-be—which perhaps she was. The baby should come first. "All right. If I stay with my sister a couple of weeks, and rest the whole time, can I come home then?"

At last Pat smiled, having gotten her way. "We'll see. It would be nice if you were within a reasonable driving distance of the hospital when you go into labor. Meanwhile, I'll get you connected to a doctor and a hospital down where your sister lives—just in case."

Keely started packing as soon as she got home. By the time the suitcase was half-full, she'd convinced herself that going away was the best course of action. Ben and Tina would have some time alone to regroup. Without the constant reminder of Keely and her enormous stomach, maybe Ben could at least be honest with himself about what he wanted from this relationship. And Keely did need a break from the physical and emotional stress. She'd been foolhardy to push herself—Pat had made her see that.

She heard Ben's car in the driveway as she put the last few items into her bag. He was early. Ever since that horrible night when she'd burned the enchiladas, he'd been making a special effort to make it home on time. After tonight, he wouldn't have to worry about that anymore.

He breezed into the bedroom as she was closing the latches on her suitcase. "There you are," he said triumphantly as he strode toward her to take his customary hello kiss, a big grin on his face. He skidded to a stop and the grin faded as his gaze locked on the suitcase. "What's this?"

Keely put on a show of false bravado. "I'm finally taking your advice," she said cheerfully. "I'm going to stay with Eileen for a while, maybe about two weeks."

Instead of the pleased response she'd expected, Ben looked as if he'd been kicked in the stomach.

"What's wrong? That's what you want me to do, isn't it?" She had decided not to tell him about her fall on the ice and her trip to the emergency room. He was such a fanatic worrier when it came to her health or the baby's. He would probably insist on checking her into the hospital if he found out about the near-disaster, no matter what assurances she gave that her condition was stable.

"It's not what *I* want, personally," he said when he found his voice. "But for your sake and the baby's, I think it's a good idea. Do you want me to drive you?"

"No, that's okay. Eileen's picking me up in the morning."

"Oh. Well, then, let me at least take you out to dinner."

It was a nice idea, but she could hear Pat's voice in her ear saying, *No way. Get to bed.* Keely shook her head. "I'm really tired. How about we order in a pizza?"

Ben made the phone call, still puzzling over this sudden change of heart. Why was Keely leaving now? He'd thought things were going along smoothly enough. Had Tina said something to upset Keely? Or had he unknowingly done something, created some kind of stress, that had convinced her that her sister's farm would be a healthier environment than her own home?

Intellectually he knew this would be good for Keely's well-being, and if she'd gone away when he'd first suggested it, he would have accepted her temporary absence. But things had changed. Now it was *her* idea. She'd made the decision to leave without even consulting him.

On a gut-instinct level, he wanted to take her by the shoulders and demand that she stay here as she'd promised. No matter how firmly he told himself that she would only be gone two weeks, he felt she was abandoning him.

Eleven

"Hey, Daddy, look at this one." Giggling, Tina held up a snapshot of herself as a baby, sitting in a splash pool, a silly grin on her face. "How old was I here?"

"Oh, about six months, I guess."

They had just finished their traditional Sunday-morning pancakes. Ben had been cleaning up the kitchen when Tina had disappeared, then reappeared with a box of old snapshots. Now she sat at the kitchen island, pulling out the pictures one by one, showing him the best ones as he loaded the dishwasher.

He paused to study another photo, one of Tina at about a year-and-a-half, clinging to his neck like a monkey. She'd been such a mischievous baby, but so full of life and love. From the time of her birth, she had been the center of Ben's existence, the source of most of his frustration, quite a bit of grief, but also a great deal of happiness.

"Ooh, look at *this* one. What an ugly dress!"

"I thought so at the time," Ben said dryly. "But you grabbed on to it as we were walking through a discount store. I couldn't talk you out of it."

"I'm glad my taste has improved."

Ben could have argued the point. His daughter was at this moment dressed in an artfully paint-spattered sweatshirt with the sleeves ripped out, a pair of holey jeans and earrings that dangled to her shoulders. At least she'd let her hair grow out a bit. "Why did you drag out these old baby pictures, anyway?" he asked.

"Oh, I don't know."

"You aren't trying to make a point of some kind?"

She hesitated. "Well, I mean, you don't seem very excited about the new baby."

"Of course I'm excited," he huffed.

"But you've hardly said anything, especially since... Daddy, when's Keely coming home? She was only s'posed to be gone two weeks, and it's been three."

"You miss her, do you?"

"Well, you have to admit she's a better cook than you."

"Tina," he began sternly, "I didn't marry Keely so she could be our cook and housekeeper."

"I know, I know." Tina chewed on her lower lip, obviously struggling with some inner storm. "Okay, yes, I miss her. And...oh, Daddy, I'm afraid I'm the reason she went away. I said some terrible things to her. And then, that night, I heard the two of you fighting. I heard Keely say something about a divorce." Tina's dark eyes were shiny with the threat of tears.

"Tina, sweetheart." Ben threw aside his dish towel and put his arms around her, nearly pulling her off her stool. "It's not your fault Keely had to leave, I promise. She just needed to rest."

Tina submitted herself to the hug for a few seconds before wiggling free. "But for how long?" she demanded.

Ben couldn't answer that.

"You're just as scared as I am that she's not coming back."

A knife twisted in his gut. Life was hell without Keely.

It had been bad enough when he thought she'd be gone only two weeks. He had talked on the phone to her almost every night, reassuring her that she should stay at Eileen's farm for as long as she needed even as he counted the days until her return. But the two-week point had come and gone, and Keely had made no mention of when she might move back home where she belonged, Ben's optimism had faded and his mood had grown progressively blacker.

Did she miss him at all? he wondered. Or was she relieved to be away from the pressures of married life? Did she lie awake at night, wishing for someone to hold her? When she did sleep, did she dream of his arms around her, only to wake and feel a disappointment so heavy it crushed the breath out of her?

"I think we should do something," Tina said.

"Like what? We can't make her come home if she doesn't want to."

"But she *has* to. If she stays at Aunt Eileen's much longer, the baby'll get born there without us. Besides, how do we know she doesn't want to come home? Maybe she's just waiting for us to ask her. I think we should *ask* her."

Ben took a deep breath. He was surprised at how disturbed he felt over the thought of that baby coming into the world without him. Every day he and Keely were separated, the possibility grew more likely. "I want Keely back as much as you do," he said, "but we can't push her right now. She's under a lot of strain. She'll come home when she's ready."

"Like Mama?"

Ben opened his mouth, but no words came out. Tina had a knack for cutting to the chase with a painfully sharp tongue.

"I don't remember much about when Mama left," she continued relentlessly, "but I do know you said that she would come home when she was ready. She never did."

He wanted to protest that this situation was entirely different. Family had meant nothing to Nora. Family was everything to Keely. She cared for him and Tina. She *loved* them . . . didn't she? But inside he was shaking so hard he couldn't speak. Tina had put his worst fears into words. How could he be so sure Keely would come back, or that she loved him? They had never spoken of love.

A few weeks ago he'd been thinking in terms of "enjoying" his marriage to Keely. Now he could see how thoroughly he'd been fooling himself. He didn't merely "enjoy" having Keely to come home to every night, to exchange the day's highs and lows, and to share those soft, secret nights with. She had become a part of him, an important part as necessary to his life as his heart and lungs. She had become so deeply ingrained in the fiber of his soul that he could feel her inside of him.

He had never told her any of that.

Tina spoke again. "*Do* something, Daddy." In her voice Ben could hear the frightened seven-year-old she'd once been, the child who had been unable to prevent her mother from leaving no matter what she said or did.

Ben felt just as powerless now. He threw up his hands in frustration. "I'd *do* something if I just knew . . . wait a minute."

"What?" The single word was fraught with hope.

"Just let me think . . ."

A sudden anger washed over him. Why was he being so indecisive about this? After his farce of a marriage with Nora had ended, he had sworn he would never let another person call all the shots and make all the decisions that affected his life. Yet that was exactly what he was allowing Keely to do.

He'd been handling her with kid gloves, afraid of pressuring her. But dammit, didn't what *he* wanted count for anything?

It was time for the gloves to come off. Keely's ambivalence was hurting him, but worse, it was hurting his daughter, and he wouldn't stand for that. He intended to tell Keely exactly where he stood and then demand that she do the same.

He looked at Tina. "Go get dressed."

"Why?"

"Because we're taking a little drive down south. And we're not coming back home until we get some results."

Tina gave a whoop as she slid off her stool and, for once, ran to do as her father had told her.

Keely shooed a cranky red hen off its nest box, where a big brown egg waited for her. "Good girl," she crooned, collecting the prize and laying it gently in a basket as the chicken looked on, clucking indignantly. Most of the other nest boxes in the small chicken coop were vacant. Keely gathered the eggs, ten in all, before an irate rooster chased her back out into the cold, pecking at her heels.

"Ouch! I get the message, I'm leaving."

She found Eileen in the kitchen, busily preparing a late lunch. Her youngest son, Jason, sat in the middle of the floor playing with the pots and pans he'd dragged out of the cabinets. The other two boys were probably tending to their chores. Even Sunday was a workday on the farm.

Eileen looked up in surprise when she saw Keely enter. "What are you doing up?" she scolded.

"Oh, Eileen, I couldn't lie in that bed another minute. I'm so sick of being idle. Look, I collected the eggs."

"Greg's gonna be pretty surprised when he goes out there later and finds all the nests empty." Greg was her middle child, seven years old and already a diligent worker. "Well, don't just stand there," Eileen continued. "If you insist on getting out of bed, at least sit down. Where did you get that awful coat?"

"I found it in the mudroom. It must be one of John's, 'cause it's the only one I could get around my middle." Keely eased herself into a chair at the big kitchen table. Her back had been killing her when she woke up this morning. She thought moving around would ease the kinks out of it, but if anything the pain was worse.

"I think I should go home," she said abruptly. "You've been wonderful, sis, but I've had about all the rest I can handle."

Eileen eyed her speculatively. "Has anything changed?"

"No," Keely admitted. She'd been hoping her separation from Ben would have some magic effect on him. Every time they talked on the phone she waited for him to say he wanted her back home. She listened to the slightest nuance in his voice that would indicate he missed her as much as she did him. But although he was unfailingly kind and concerned, he also made a point of stressing how important it was that she take it easy, and that she should stay with Eileen for as long as she needed to.

Hardly the attitude she'd hoped for.

"I guess you can't stay here much longer," Eileen conceded, "not if you want to have the baby in Kansas City. How much longer? Three weeks?"

"Three weeks!" Keely echoed, her voice full of disgust. If she'd known how uncomfortable carrying a kid could be . . . she still would have gladly done it, of course.

"If you really want to go, I'll drive you. But only if you promise to take it easy. If you make yourself too useful you'll be right back where you were when you came here. Do you have any idea how crummy you looked when you first arrived?"

"I did?"

"You were as white as that snow on the ground out there, and you had purple circles under your eyes. You look much better now."

"Physically, maybe," Keely conceded. "But I miss Ben. I even miss Tina, the brat. I don't know if they miss me, though."

Eileen listened as she peeled potatoes at the sink, but her attention was directed out the window. Her hands stilled. "I think you're about to get your answer. There's a navy blue Porsche coming up the driveway."

"You're kidding." Keely's heart thumped wildly as she lumbered out of her chair to join Eileen at the window. Sure enough, it was Ben's car. "Omigod, I must look awful!" she wailed, running frantic fingers through her hair. She was wearing a horrible old flannel shirt and a pair of Eileen's cast-off maternity sweatpants. Good Lord, she would probably scare Ben right back to Kansas City.

"You look fine," Eileen soothed.

"What's he doing here?" Keely watched him get out of the car. He looked typically sexy and gorgeous, wrapped in a worn shearling jacket and soft blue corduroys. But his expression was stern—grim, even.

She did a double-take when she saw Tina climbing out of the passenger side.

"I don't imagine they're here to buy eggs," Eileen quipped. "Don't just stand there like a ninny. Invite them in for lunch."

Her legs wobbly with nerves, Keely went to the front door. She would at least ask them in out of the cold, though she was dubious about the lunch idea. Ben didn't look to be in a socializing mood.

She opened the door before he had a chance to knock. She and Ben stood staring at each other for several heartbeats, until at last his face broke into a smile. "Well, if you aren't a sight for sore eyes."

"I'm a sight, all right," she said with an answering grin. She opened the door wider. They stomped the snow off their boots and came into Eileen's big, friendly living room. Then they all stood and stared at each other some more.

The tension was broken as Jason toddled in to inspect the newcomers.

Tina grabbed at the distraction. "Jason! You're so big! Do you remember me, your cousin Tina?" She scooped the two-year-old up and onto one hip like a pro. Jason's eyes widened, but he didn't object. When Tina looked back at Keely, she smiled with embarrassment, as if she'd just revealed how uncool she was by *goo-gooing* over a child.

"I just have one thing to say," Tina began suddenly, and then launched into what was obviously a well-rehearsed speech. "I'm sorry if I said anything that made you feel like I didn't want you around. I miss you, and if you come home I'll eat dinner with you guys every night for a month."

Quite a concession, Keely marveled, struggling not to smile.

"And?" Ben prompted.

"Oh, yeah, and I'll even *cook* dinner if you'll tell me how and... and I really did like your Christmas decorations." She looked at her father. "Okay, Daddy, the rest is up to you." Jason chose that moment to yank Tina's hair. "Ow. You keep that up, kid, and I'll have to shave my head again. Let's you and me go find your mom, huh?" She wandered toward the kitchen, leaving Ben and Keely alone.

"So, what are you doing here?" Keely asked as she sank into a faded chintz sofa. She kept her tone light and conversational, not wanting to reveal what a mass of anxiety she was inside—or how important his answer was.

His stern expression had returned. "I'm here to bring you home. I will *not* allow you to give birth to my child a hundred and fifty miles away from me."

"Okay," she said meekly, though inside she was jumping for joy.

"You've been hiding out for long enough. It's time you came home and faced your responsibilities. You married me for better or worse, and I'm about to get a whole lot worse unless you pack your bags right now."

"Okay, fine." She wasn't sure why he was angry, but she didn't mind. It was a welcome relief from the way he'd been walking on eggs the past few months. Finally an honest emotional reaction.

"I don't want to hear any arguments. Your place is—"

"Ben, I said okay!" she yelled, breaking through his tirade.

"Then why are you just sitting there? Go pack!"

"I will—soon as I figure out how to get up from this sofa. I seem to be stuck."

Ben's ire melted. With a smile that made her go warm inside, he took both her hands and gently helped her to her feet. But instead of letting her go, he pulled her closer—as close as her huge stomach would allow—and gave her a passionate, welcoming kiss. She knew then that he hadn't really been angry with her.

"Oh, my," she said on an uneven breath when he released her. "You *did* miss me." She packed in record time.

Ben glanced over at Keely, who dozed peacefully in the seat next to him. Tina, too, was asleep, curled into an impossible knot in the tiny back seat.

They were almost home. As soon as they arrived, he planned to put Keely into bed and pamper her mercilessly, so she would never want to take a vacation away from him again. Then he would tell her all the things he'd held back—things he hadn't even admitted to himself until recently. She would never have any reason to doubt that he wanted and loved this baby—and her.

The baby, however, had different plans.

"Ben?" Keely said calmly as the Kansas City skyline came into view. "I think we'd better head for the hospital."

"Why? What's wrong?" With great effort, he managed to keep from driving into a ditch as his heart rose into his throat.

"Nothing's wrong, except I think I'm having a baby."

"Now? You're having contractions? I thought you were asleep!"

"I was, sort of. But I've been having these pains for the past couple of hours—"

"Couple of hours! Why didn't you say something?"

"Because I didn't want to scare you. I could just see you driving ninety miles an hour all the way to Kansas City— look, you're doing it now," she cautioned, glancing at the speedometer. "Don't worry, there's plenty of time."

Ben eased up on the accelerator. "I'm glad we took those Lamaze classes, except I'm the one who needs the relaxation techniques." He was trembling all the way down to his boots. "For God's sake, Keely, how can you be so calm? You're three weeks early!"

"I know, but I went to see Eileen's obstetrician a couple of days ago, and he said I could expect it to happen any time. The baby is large and strong, and—*oof!*" She grabbed Ben's hand and squeezed it hard as her face contorted with pain.

"*Keely!*"

"It's okay," she said as she loosened her iron grip. "That one was a little stronger than the others have been."

Tina's head popped up from the back seat. "What's going on?"

"I'm in labor," Keely said casually.

"Cool!"

"Not really. I hate going to the hospital looking like I escaped from a refugee camp. Maybe we could stop at home first so I can change."

"No way!" Ben couldn't *believe* her nerve.

Unperturbed, she started rummaging around in her purse. "Well, I can at least put some makeup on."

"Makeup? To have a baby?"

Despite his objections, by the time they reached the hospital Keely had made up her face and filed her fingernails.

The next few minutes were a whirlwind of admission procedures. All the while, Ben's stomach churned with a mixture of fear and anticipation. He wasn't ready for this. He'd thought there was plenty of time to prepare himself.

A nurse put Keely into a wheelchair and took her away from him, much to his distress. Then he and Tina were shown to the "birthing room."

"She's gonna have the baby *here?*" Tina asked in amazement.

"I guess so." The room wasn't exactly what Ben had envisioned, either. It looked like someone's tastefully furnished living room. He remembered Keely telling him something of what to expect from the family-centered maternity program, but the room was still a surprise.

"Did you watch when I was born?" Tina asked.

"Uh-huh."

"How was it?"

"It was...educational." And kind of scary. "You don't have to stay if it makes you uncomfortable, you know."

"Okay. I'll see how it goes."

When Keely was wheeled into the room on a peculiar-looking rolling bed, she wore a flowered gown and a scowl. "They made me wash my face," she announced with obvious disgust as an orderly situated her in the middle of the room.

"You look beautiful," Ben argued. He knew he had a silly grin on his face.

"And I talked to Pat. She said that since the baby's premature, she wants to take me to a regular delivery room, so they'll have everything they need close at hand in case there's a problem."

"What problems does she expect?" Ben asked, his face coming to the forefront again. Tina frowned, too, listening intently.

"Ben, don't worry. This baby is strong and perfect. I know it. He's been kicking up a storm."

"He?" Ben narrowed his gaze suspiciously. "You said you didn't know what sex it was."

"I don't. Pat couldn't tell from the sonogram. I'm just tired of calling the baby 'it.' And speaking of what to call it, you were supposed to be thinking of names while I was—'' She gasped as another contraction hit.

"Breathe, honey," Ben urged, wrapping her hand around his so she could squeeze. "That's it. Don't fight it. It'll be over in a minute."

"Don't fight it?" she said when the pain had passed. "Easy for you to say."

For the next few hours, Ben and Tina took turns trying to distract Keely from the pain. They read her amusing stories from magazines, told terrible jokes and argued amiably over dozens of names. They finally narrowed the field down to six—Rose, Carrie, or Bonnie for a girl, and Max, Spencer, or Matthew for a boy. They fed her ice chips. But Keely showed amazingly little appreciation for their efforts. In fact, she was in a decidedly bad humor for someone about to experience the moment she'd waited a lifetime for. And most of her ill will was directed toward Ben.

"This is all your fault," she grumbled between contractions. "You're the one who got me into this mess."

"I don't recall your complaining at the time," he quipped, right in front of the nurse who was checking on Keely's progress.

The nurse smiled indulgently. "Don't worry," she assured Ben, "she'll be in a better mood when it's all over and she holds that baby in her arms."

He fervently hoped so. The ill-humored termagant lying in the bed wasn't the stoic, optimistic Keely he knew. Then again, he wasn't sure he could do much better in her position. Not for the first time, he was eternally grateful he'd been born male.

Later in the day Pat McCommas arrived to check on Keely. Keely didn't spare the doctor from her acid tongue.

"It's about time you got here," she groused. "I want drugs."

"My, my, we are in a snit," Pat replied as she listened to the baby's heartbeat with a stethoscope. "What happened to natural childbirth?"

"That was before I knew how much it would *hurt* oh, damn!" Another contraction seized her. "Just . . . a mild . . . painkiller . . . please?"

Pat's forehead creased with compassion. "Of course, Keely, I'll go get it right now."

When Pat had gone, Keely offered a watery smile to Ben. "I'm not being a very good sport about this, am I?"

"You're being wonderful," he lied.

"Where's Tina?"

"Are you kidding? She fled at the first sign of real pain. She's squeamish, you know."

"So much for family-centered maternity." Keely cast worried eyes up at Ben. "You're not squeamish, are you?"

He squeezed her hand. "I'm here for the duration."

"Good."

The next contraction seemed a little easier. She didn't turn the air blue, anyway. When it passed, she said, "You know, I always thought that if I could just have a baby, my life would be perfect. I *am* happy about it, of course, but nothing about this pregnancy has gone according to plan—including the delivery. I thought I would be brave, and that the joy of giving birth would completely overshadow the pain."

"How could it?" Ben asked. "There's been a lot of pain and doubt to overcome."

She appraised him silently. He saw the understanding in her eyes—she knew he wasn't talking about just physical pain.

He didn't have much more time. There were things he had to say, and now was as good a time as any. At least he had a captive audience.

"From the day you first told me you were pregnant," he began, "I've been terrified. It's a frightening responsibility, raising a child. I know from experience."

As if on cue, Tina poked her head inside the door. "Hi, is everything going okay?" She wore a construction-paper chain around her neck and stickers of sailboats on her cheeks.

Ben decided not to even ask.

"Everything's fine," Keely said, feeling ashamed for having frightened the girl away with her pitiful howls of pain. "You can come back in. I'm okay, I promise."

"No, thanks." Tina disappeared.

"A frightening responsibility," Ben repeated.

"You've raised a marvelous child, an exceptional one."

Ben's eyebrows flew up. "This, from a woman who accused me of spoiling my daughter rotten?"

Keely's face flushed. "That was a long time ago, before I saw the two of you together. You're a good father."

Ben shrugged. "I try. But I've spent a lot of time wondering why fate chose to throw parenthood at me a second time, at this stage of my life. I also wondered if I would be equal to the task—if I could be the kind of father you want for your kid."

"Ben, I couldn't wish for a better father than you...as long as you..." She bit her lip, and not because of a contraction.

"As long as I what?"

She hesitated, then plunged ahead. "Well, I couldn't ask for a more responsible parent. I know you'll always do what's right by this child. But I was kind of hoping you really wanted it, too."

Ben bristled like an irate porcupine. "Of course I want it! I may have doubts about myself, but I never, ever, wished that the child hadn't been conceived. Not once."

"I believe you, Ben. You don't have to shake the hospital down telling me."

"Sorry," he said in a more reasonable voice. "I guess I didn't realize what a jerk you thought I was."

"I never thought you were a jerk. I just didn't know how you felt—about anything. You've been so neutral. I was afraid you regretted that hasty wedding."

"Why would I regret it when it was my idea? I might have been a little scared, like I said, but you two—" he lovingly caressed her abdomen "—wound yourselves right around my heart." And any hopes he'd had of remaining detached had long since fled. He was in as deep as a man could get.

"Do you really mean that? It seemed like you didn't even miss me while I was gone."

"I'm a good actor. Believe me, I was miserable, I just didn't want to pressure you. Make no mistake, I love you and I love the baby, and I plan to love the both of you for a lifetime. It just took me a while to admit it."

The loveliest, most dreamy expression came over Keely's face. "I love you, too, Ben, with all my heart."

A wonderful peacefulness settled over Keely. Why had the words been so difficult to say? Another contraction hit. She panted as she'd been taught in her Lamaze class. It wasn't so bad.

A nurse entered with a syringe on a tray.

"Ick, is that for me?" Keely asked.

The nurse smiled. "It's your painkiller."

"I don't want it. The kid's almost here. If I've gotten this far without drugs, I should be able to do the rest."

The nurse shrugged. "Whatever."

The rest of Keely's labor passed in a giddy, pain-hazy sort of blur—kind of like her wedding. She remembered a few of the sharper images—the faces of the nurses as they watched the baby's progress into the world; Pat's voice, urging her to push; the moment of elation when she heard the hearty first cries.

Mostly she remembered Ben in his sterile gown and mask, looking a little green but sticking by her side through it all, holding her hand. When he held his new daughter for the first time, his eyes were so full of love, for the baby and for Keely, that she knew she would never again doubt him.

"April," he said.

"Pardon me?"

"We'll call her April, for the month we met."

That particular name had never been a contender. But the notion was so romantic, Keely immediately agreed. "April it is."

She would always think of April as their own private miracle. Now, her name would be a joyful reminder of the day Keely had burst into Ben Kinkaid's life, intent on teaching him a few things about being a responsible father. Instead they had both learned lessons of love, commitment and parenthood that would last them a lifetime.

*   *   *   *   *

NORA ROBERTS

Love has a language all its own, and for centuries flowers have symbolized love's finest expression. Discover the language of flowers—and love—in this romantic collection of 48 favorite books by bestselling author Nora Roberts.

Two titles are available every other month at your favorite retail outlet.

In August, look for:

The Name of the Game, Volume #33
A Will and a Way, Volume #34

In October, look for:

Affaire Royale, Volume #35
Less of a Stranger, Volume #36

Collect all 48 titles and become fluent in

THE LANGUAGE of LOVE

Silhouette® ™

MEN MADE IN AMERICA

Fifty red-blooded, white-hot, true-blue hunks from every State in the Union!

Beginning in May, look for MEN MADE IN AMERICA! Written by some of our most popular authors, these stories feature fifty of the strongest, sexiest men, each from a different state in the union!

Two titles available every other month at your favorite retail outlet.

In July, look for:

CALL IT DESTINY by Jayne Ann Krentz (Arizona)
ANOTHER KIND OF LOVE by Mary Lynn Baxter (Arkansas)

In September, look for:

DECEPTIONS by Annette Broadrick (California)
STORMWALKER by Dallas Schulze (Colorado)

You won't be able to resist MEN MADE IN AMERICA!

If you've been looking for something a little bit different and a little bit spooky, let Silhouette Books take you on a journey to the dark side of love with

Every month, Silhouette will bring you two romantic, spine-tingling Shadows novels, written by some of your favorite authors, such as *New York Times* bestselling author Heather Graham Pozzessere, Anne Stuart, Helen R. Myers and Rachel Lee—to name just a few.

In July, look for:
HEART OF THE BEAST by Carla Cassidy
DARK ENCHANTMENT by Jane Toombs

In August, look for:
A SILENCE OF DREAMS by Barbara Faith
THE SEVENTH NIGHT by Amanda Stevens

In September, look for:
FOOTSTEPS IN THE NIGHT by Lee Karr
WHAT WAITS BELOW by Jane Toombs

*Come into the world of Shadows and prepare
to tremble with fear—and passion....*

Silhouette Books
is proud to present
our best authors,
their best books...
and the best in
your reading pleasure!

Throughout 1993, look for exciting
books by these top names in
contemporary romance:

DIANA PALMER—
Fire and Ice in June

ELIZABETH LOWELL—
Fever in July

CATHERINE COULTER—
Afterglow in August

LINDA HOWARD—
Come Lie With Me in September

When it comes to passion,
we wrote the book.

BOBT2

SILHOUETTE® Desire®

RED, WHITE AND BLUE...
Six sexy, hardworking, hometown hunks who were born and bred in the USA!

NEED PROTECTION?
Then you must read ZEKE #793 by Annette Broadrick
July's Man of the Month

NEED TO TAKE THE PLUNGE?
Then dive into BEN #794 by Karen Leabo

NEED TO GET AWAY?
Then sail away with DEREK #795 by Leslie Davis Guccione

NEED TO FIND YOUR ROOTS?
Then dig into CAMERON #796 by Beverly Barton

NEED A MAN?
Then warm up with JAKE #797 by Helen R. Myers

NEED A HAND?
Then you need to meet WILL #798 by Kelly Jamison

Desire invites you to meet these sexy, down-home guys! These hunks are HOT and will make you pledge allegiance to the all-American man!

SDRWB